I'M GONE

Also by Jean Echenoz

Cherokee

Double Jeopardy

Plan of Occupancy

Big Blondes (The New Press)

I'M GONE

A NOVEL

JEAN ECHENOZ

Translated from the French by Mark Polizzotti

THE NEW PRESS

NEW YORK

Originally published in France as *Je m'en vais*
by Les Éditions de Minuit, Paris, 1999
Published in the United States by The New Press, New York, 2001
Distributed by W. W. Norton & Company, Inc., New York

LIBRARY OF CONGRESS CATALOGING-IN-PUBLICATION DATA

Echenoz, Jean.
    [Je m'en vais. English]
    I'm gone : a novel / Jean Echenoz ; translated by
Mark Polizzotti.
        p.   cm.
    ISBN 1-56584-628-1 (hc.)
    I. Polizzotti, Mark.   II. Title.

PQ2665.C5 J413 2001
843'.914—dc21   00-064601

The New Press was established in 1990 as a not-for-profit alternative to the large, commercial publishing houses currently dominating the book publishing industry. The New Press operates in the public interest rather than for private gain, and is committed to publishing, in innovative ways, works of educational, cultural, and community value that are often deemed insufficiently profitable.

The New Press
450 West 41st Street, 6th floor
New York, NY 10036
www.thenewpress.com

Printed in the United States of America

2   4   6   8   10   9   7   5   3   1

I'M GONE

"I'm going," said Ferrer. "I'm leaving you. You can keep everything, but I'm gone." And as Suzanne's gaze drifted toward the floor, settling for no good reason on an electrical outlet, Felix Ferrer dropped his keys on the entryway table. Then he buttoned up his overcoat and walked out, gently shutting the front door behind him.

Outside, without a glance at Suzanne's car whose fogged-up windows kept silent beneath the streetlamps, Ferrer began walking the six hundred yards toward the Corentin-Celton metro stop. At nearly nine o'clock, this first Sunday evening in January, the train was all but deserted. Only a dozen men were inside, unattached, as Ferrer seemed to have become in the last twenty-five minutes. Normally he would have rejoiced to find two empty facing benches, like a little compartment for himself alone, which in the metro was his preferred seating arrangement. But on this evening he scarcely gave it a thought, distracted but less preoccupied than he would have imagined by the scene that had just been played out with Suzanne, a woman of difficult character. Having envisioned a more vehement response, cries interspersed with threats and fiery insults, he was relieved, but somewhat put out by his own relief.

He set down his valise, which contained mainly toilet articles and a change of underwear, and at first he stared straight ahead, mechanically skimming over the advertising panels for floor coverings, dating services, and real estate listings. Later, between the Vaugirard and Volontaires stations, Ferrer opened the valise to remove an auction catalogue featuring traditional Persian artwork, which he leafed through up to Madeleine, where he got off.

Around the Madeleine church, strings of unlit Christmas lights hovered above streets still more deserted than the subway. The decorated windows of the high-priced shops reminded the nonexistent pedestrians that they would survive the end-of-year festivities. Alone in his overcoat, Ferrer skirted the church toward an even number on Rue de l'Arcade.

To find the building's entry code, his hands forged a path under his clothing: the left one toward the address book slipped into an inside pocket, the right toward his glasses stuffed into a breast pocket. Then, having passed through the main door, ignoring the elevator, he firmly attacked the service stairs. He reached the sixth floor less out of breath than I would have imagined, in front of a badly repainted brick-red door whose hinges bespoke at least two attempted break-ins. No name on the door, just a tacked-up photo curling at the corners, depicting the lifeless body of Manuel Montoliu, an ex-matador-cum-banderillero, after an animal named Cubatisto had opened his heart like a book on May 1, 1992: Ferrer tapped lightly on the photo twice.

While he waited, the nails of his right hand dug into

the inner surface of his left forearm, just above the wrist, where numerous tendons and blue veins intersected under whiter skin. Then, her hair very dark and very long, no older than thirty nor shorter than five foot ten, the young woman named Laurence who had just opened the door smiled at him without saying a word before closing it behind them both. And the next morning at around ten, Ferrer left for his studio.

2

Six months later, also at around ten, the same Felix
Ferrer climbed out of a taxi in front of Terminal B at
Roissy-Charles de Gaulle Airport, under a naive June
sun in a partly overcast sky. As Ferrer was quite early,
check-in hadn't yet begun for his flight: for three-
quarters of an hour he had to pace the corridors, pushing a cart laden with a carry-on bag, a suitcase, and
his overcoat, which had become rather heavy for the
season. He had another coffee, bought a packet of
Kleenex and a box of effervescent aspirin tablets, then
looked for a quiet spot where he could wait in peace.

If he had a hard time finding one, it's because an
airport does not really exist in and of itself. It's only a
place of passage, an airlock, a fragile facade in the
middle of an open field, a belvedere circled by runways
where rabbits with kerosene breath leap and bound, a
turntable infested by winds that carry a host of cor-
puscles of myriad origins: grains of sand from every
desert, flecks of gold and mica from every river, volca-
nic or radioactive dust, pollens and viruses, rice powder and cigar ash. Finding a quiet corner amid all that
is not the easiest thing in the world, but Ferrer finally
discovered an ecumenical chapel in the basement of the
terminal, in whose armchairs one could reflect calmly
on nothing much at all. He killed a little time there

before checking his bags and wandering around the duty-free area, where he purchased neither alcohol nor tobacco nor perfume, nor anything else. He was not going on vacation. No point in weighing himself down. At shortly before one in the afternoon he boarded a DC-10 in which celestial music, turned as low as possible to pacify the clientele, accompanied him as he took his seat. Ferrer folded his coat, shoved it with his carry-on into the overhead compartment, then, installed in the minuscule square yard allotted him next to a window, he began settling in: seatbelt fastened, newspapers and magazines arranged before him, glasses and sleeping pill within reach. As the seat next to him was fortunately unoccupied, he adopted it as an annex.

Then it's always the same story: you wait; your inattentive ear listens to the prerecorded announcements, your eye absently follows the safety demonstrations. The vehicle finally sets in motion, imperceptibly at first then faster and faster until you take off, heading northwest toward clouds you then pass through. Below these clouds, later on, leaning against his window, Ferrer makes out an expanse of ocean, decorated with an island he can't identify; then an expanse of land with a lake in the middle, whose name he doesn't know. He dozes off; he casually watches several opening credits of movies that he has trouble following to the end, distracted by the comings and goings of the stewardesses who aren't what they used to be. He is totally alone.

Amid two hundred people pressed into a cabin, you

are in fact more isolated than ever. This passive solitude, you think, might provide a good opportunity to take stock of your life, to reflect on the meaning of the things that go into it. You try for a moment, you even force yourself a bit, but you don't struggle for long against the disjointed internal monologue that surfaces, and so you let it drop. You curl up and get drowsy; you'd really like to sleep. You ask the stewardess for a drink, which will help you sleep better; then you ask for another to help you swallow the sleeping pill: you sleep.

In Montreal, as he got off the DC-10, the airport workers seemed unusually dispersed under a sky that was wider than other skies, then the Greyhound bus was longer than other buses, but the highway was of normal size. Arriving in Quebec, Ferrer took a Subaru taxi toward the port, Coast Guard division, Pier 11. The taxi dropped him in front of a slate bearing the notice in chalk, *Destination: Arctic*, and two hours later the ice breaker NCGC *Des Groseilliers* was heading toward the Great North.

For five years, until the January evening when he'd left the house in Issy, all of Felix Ferrer's days except Sundays had been spent in exactly the same way. Up at seven-thirty; ten minutes in the toilet with some kind of printed matter, from a treatise on aesthetics to a humble flyer; then preparing a breakfast for Suzanne and himself that was scientifically balanced in vitamins and mineral salts. Next, twenty minutes of gymnastics while he listened to the news on the radio. After that, he woke Suzanne and aired out the house.

After which, in the bathroom, Ferrer brushed his teeth to the point of hemorrhage without ever looking at himself in the mirror, letting two and a half gallons of cold city water run for no reason. He always washed in the same order, inalterably from left to right and top to bottom. He always shaved in the same order, inalterably right cheek then left cheek, chin, lower then upper lip, neck. And since Ferrer, subject to these immutable orders, asked himself every morning how to break out of this ritual, the question itself became incorporated into the ritual. Without ever managing to resolve it, at nine o'clock he left for his studio.

What he called his studio wasn't really a studio. It was kind of one when Ferrer had called himself an artist and considered himself a sculptor; these days it was nothing more than the back room of his gallery, which could also serve as a one-room apartment now that he had gone into dealing other people's art. It was on the ground floor of a small building in the 9th arrondissement, on a street that seemed unlikely to contain a gallery: a lively merchant artery, rather working-class for the neighborhood. Just opposite the gallery a large scaffolding was going up, which was only in the beginning stages; for the moment they were digging deep foundations. Ferrer arrived and brewed some coffee, downed two Efferalgan, opened his mail, most of which he threw out, toyed with the paperwork lying around, and waited for ten o'clock, struggling valiantly against the notion of a first cigarette. Then he opened the gallery and made several phone calls. At around twelve-ten, still by phone, he cast about for someone to have lunch with: he always found someone.

Beginning at three o'clock and for the rest of the afternoon, Ferrer manned the gallery; then at seven-thirty he called Suzanne, invariably in the same vein: don't wait for me for dinner. She always waited and, at ten-thirty, Ferrer was in bed with her, domestic squabble every other evening, then lights out at eleven. And for five years, yes, things had gone this way before changing abruptly last January 3. Still, not everything had changed: not without some dismay, Ferrer was forced to admit, for example, that in Laurence's narrow bathroom he continued to wash from left to right and top to bottom. But he wouldn't stay at her place for long; one of these days he would return to live in his studio.

Always several vacuumings behind, this studio looked a lot like a bachelor pad, or the lair of a hunted criminal, or a disused legacy while the heirs were fighting it out in court. Five sticks of furniture supplied minimum comfort, alongside a small safe whose combination Ferrer had long ago forgotten, and the three-by-nine kitchen contained a stove dotted with stains, a refrigerator empty save for two wilted vegetables, shelves supporting preserves well past expiration. As the refrigerator was rarely used, a natural iceberg invaded the freezer; every year, when the iceberg neared floe proportions, Ferrer defrosted it with a hair dryer and a bread knife. Tartar, saltpeter, and purulent plaster had colonized the chiaroscuro of the bathroom, but a closet concealed six dark-colored suits, a procession of white shirts, and a battery of neckties. This was because Ferrer, when he looked after his gallery, made a point of being impeccably dressed: the strict, almost austere outfit of a politician or bank manager.

In what passed for his living room, there was nothing to recall the gallery owner's past artistic ambitions, aside from two exhibition posters from Heidelberg and Montpellier—and aside from two blocks of marble, chiseled and left in disgrace, now serving as a low table or television stand; keeping for themselves, in their heart of hearts, the forms that had once been intended to surge from their loins. These might have been a skull, a fountain, a nude, but Ferrer had given up first.

Now it was an ice breaker one hundred yards long and twenty wide: eight coupled engines with a combined 13,600 horsepower, maximum speed 16.20 knots, 24-foot draft. They had settled Ferrer in his cabin: furniture bolted to the decks, sink with pedal-controlled faucet, TV screwed into an extension of the single bunk, and Bible in the nightstand drawer. Plus a small fan, paradoxical given that the heat was at the highest setting, maintaining a canicular 85° F., as in all polar outfittings, whether for ships, tractor cabs, or buildings. Ferrer arranged his belongings in the wardrobe, setting within reach, near his bunk, a book on Inuit sculpture.

The crew of the *Des Groseilliers* was comprised of fifty men, as well as three women whom Ferrer noticed immediately: a ruddy, compact young thing in charge of the mooring lines, a nail-biter who looked after the accounts, and a nurse with an ideal nurse's physique, discreetly made-up, delicately tanned, barely dressed beneath her blouse, who also ran the book and video libraries and was named Brigitte. As Ferrer would soon acquire the habit of borrowing books and videos from her, it took him only a few days to understand that Brigitte, when night fell, went to join a radio operator with square chin, spindle-shaped nose, and handlebar mustache. Not much hope in that regard, but we'd see, we'd see, it wasn't over yet.

On the first day, on the bridge, Ferrer met the officers. The captain looked like an actor and his executive officer like a master of ceremonies, but that's as far as it went: the other officers, senior or junior, didn't remind him of anyone in particular. After introductions were made they found little to say to each other; Ferrer went off to explore the vast warm body of the ice breaker, progressively tempted by its smells. At first it was clean and didn't smell like anything, but if you sniffed a little harder you made out, in order of appearance, olfactory ghosts of diesel fuel, burnt fat, tobacco, vomit, and compacted garbage; then with a little more effort, a vague, floating undertone of dirty or moldy dampness, briny evacuation, last gasp of the sewage pipe.

Loudspeakers buzzed orders, guys joked around behind half-open doors. Along the passageways, Ferrer came across, without speaking to them, various crewmen, stewards and mechanics unused to the presence of nonprofessionals and in any case too busy to care: apart from their duties in the navigational operations, most worked all day in huge mechanical or electrical workshops located on the ship's lower decks, stuffed with enormous machine tools and tiny delicate instruments. Ferrer managed to chat a bit with a shy, vulnerable, musclebound young sailor who drew his attention to several passing birds. The ptarmigan, for example, the eider that eiderdown comes from, the fulmar, the petrel, and I think that's about it.

That was about it. The fatty meals were served at set times and they were allowed only a brief half hour at the bar, every evening, to buy themselves a beer or two. After that first day of discovery, the weather turned foggy and began to deteriorate. Through the porthole of his cabin, Ferrer saw Newfoundland parade by on his right before they began to skirt the coast of Labrador up to Davis Inlet, then to the Hudson Strait, without once hearing an engine rumble.

Bathing tall cliffs in a violet brown-ochre, the still air was icy, and therefore heavy, crushing its full weight onto an equally still sea of sandy yellow-gray: no gust of wind, no boats, soon not even any birds to animate it with the slightest movement, no sound. Deserted, spotted with mosses and lichens like badly shaven cheeks, the coasts fell sharply straight into the water. Through the uniform fog they divined, more than they saw, the flanks of glaciers detach and fall at imperceptible speed. The silence remained perfect until they met the ice floe.

As it was relatively thin at first, the ice breaker began to slice a path through its front. Soon it became too thick to keep on. At that point the breaker rode on top of it, tried to crush it with all its weight; then the ice exploded, cracking in every direction as far as the eye could see. Down in the ship's bow, separated from the impact by two and a half inches of steel, Ferrer listened from up close to the sound it made: sound track for a haunted castle full of scraping noises, whistles, and growls, bass notes and creaking of all kinds. But back up on the bridge, he saw no more than a slight permanent crackling, like a fabric tearing easily above nuclear submarines sitting calm, silent, and still on the ocean floor, in which men cheat at cards while waiting in vain for their counterorders.

They continued on; the days passed. They came across no one, except, once, another ice breaker of the same model. They stopped alongside each other for an hour, started up again after the captains had exchanged notes and plottings, but that was all. These are territories where no one ever goes, even though a fair number of countries have more or less laid claim to them: Scandinavia, since it provided the region's first explorers; Russia, because it isn't very far; Canada, because it's nearby; and the United States, because it's the United States. Two or three times they spotted abandoned villages on the shores of Labrador, originally built by the central government for the native populations and equipped with everything from power plants to churches. But as these villages were ill adapted to the needs of the locals, the latter had destroyed them before going off somewhere else to commit suicide. Here and there near the disemboweled shacks one could still find desiccated seal carcasses hung from gibbets, the remains of food reserves protected from polar bears.

It was fascinating, it was empty and spectacular, but after a few days it also got a bit boring. It was then that Ferrer became a regular at the library, checking out classics of polar exploration—Greely, Nansen, Barents, Nordenskiöld—and videos of all types: *Rio Bravo* and *Kiss Me Deadly*, of course, but also *Kinky Cashiers* and *The Nurse Is Ready*. These latter works he borrowed only after making sure of the relations between Brigitte and the radioman; at that point, nurturing few hopes about his chances with the nurse, he had nothing to lose by degrading himself in her eyes. Vain scruples: it was with an equable smile, full of maternal indulgence, that Brigitte indifferently recorded in her register the loan of *Four Horsemen of the Apocalypse* or *Stuff Us Good*. A smile so pacifying and permissive that Ferrer soon stopped inventing daily excuses (headaches, back pains) to go ask for care (compresses, massages). As a first step, it seemed to be working.

5

What wasn't working so well, six months earlier, was business at the gallery. In the period I'm describing, the art market was nothing to write home about, and while we're on the subject, Ferrer's last electrocardiogram was nothing to write home about either. He had already had several warnings, a slight infarction whose only consequence was to make him give up tobacco, a point on which the specialist Feldman had proven intractable. If life punctuated by Marlboros had seemed like climbing a knotted rope, from that point on life without cigarettes was like climbing endlessly up an unvaryingly slippery rope.

Over the past several years, Ferrer had built himself a small stable of artists whom he regularly visited, occasionally advised, and quite clearly annoyed. There were no sculptors, given his background, but naturally some painters, like Beucler, Spontini, Gourdel, and especially Martinov—who was rather visible these days and worked only in yellow—as well as a few plastic artists. Eliseo Schwartz, for example, who, specializing in extreme temperatures, had invented closed-circuit air blowers ("Why not add valves?" Ferrer suggested. "A valve or two here and there?"); or Charles Estrellas, who haphazardly installed little hillocks of glazed sugar and talcum powder ("It could use a bit of color," hazarded Ferrer, "couldn't it?"); Marie-Nicole Guimard, who dealt in blow-ups of insect bites ("You wouldn't be interested in the same kind of thing with caterpillars?" Ferrer imagined. "Or snakes?"); and Rajputek Fracnatz, who worked exclusively on sleep ("Still, easy with the barbiturates," worried Ferrer). But in the first place, no one really wanted these works anymore these days, on top of which the artists, especially Rajputek, startled once too often out of his slumber, ended up making Ferrer understand how inopportune his visits were.

In any case, none of it sold that well anymore. Gone were the days when the telephones rang themselves hoarse, when the fax machines spewed continuous requests, when galleries the world over asked for news of his artists, statements from his artists, biographies and photos of his artists, catalogues and exhibit proposals for his artists. There had been several feverish, rather enjoyable years, when it wasn't a problem to take care of all those artists, find them grants in Berlin, foundations in Florida, or classes to teach in Strasbourg or Nancy. But the vogue for all that seemed past and the lode exhausted.

Unable to convince enough collectors to buy these works, while also noting that ethnic art was gaining ground, Ferrer had ended up revising his plan of action some time before. Gradually abandoning the plastic artists, he naturally continued to deal with the painters, especially Gourdel and Martinov—the latter in full expansion, the former clearly in decline—but he was now envisioning diverting the bulk of his efforts to more traditional channels: Bambara art, Bantu art, art of the Plains Indians—that sort of thing. To advise him in his investments, he had secured the services of a competent informant named Delahaye, who also, three afternoons per week, manned the gallery. Despite Delahaye's professional qualities, his appearance did not work to his advantage. Delahaye was a man made entirely of curves. Hunched spine, gutless face, and an asymmetrical, uncultivated mustache that spottily masked his entire upper lip and curled into his mouth; certain hairs even slipped backward up his nostrils. It was too long, it looked fake; you'd think it was glued on. Delahaye's gestures were undulating, rounded; his thinking was as sinuous as his gait; even the lenses of his eyeglasses did not reside on the same level, as the stems of his eyeglasses were twisted—in short, nothing about him was rectilinear. "Stand up straighter, Delahaye," an annoyed Ferrer sometimes told him. The other did nothing of the kind. Oh well.

In the first months following his departure from the house in Issy, Ferrer had indeed benefited from the new order in his life. Having at his disposal a towel, a bowl, and half a closet at Laurence's, at first he spent every night with her on Rue de l'Arcade. And then, little by little, things fell apart: it became no more than every other night, then every third, soon every fourth. Ferrer spent the others at the gallery, first alone, then less alone, until the day Laurence: "You're going, now," she told him. "Out. Grab your things and beat it."

"Right, fine," said Ferrer (and anyway, deep down, I don't give a shit). But after a cold night alone in the back room of the gallery, he was up early the next morning walking through the door of the nearest real estate office. That miserable studio had lasted long enough. They offered to show him a very different apartment on Rue d'Amsterdam. "It's typical Haussmann, you know?" the agent said. "Moldings on the ceiling, herringbone floors, double living room and large foyer, double glass doors, tall mirrors on the marble mantelpiece, huge hallways, maid's room, three months' security." "Right, fine," said Ferrer (I'll take it).

He moved in; by the end of the week he had bought some furniture and had the plumbing fixed. One evening, as he was finally feeling at home in one of his brand-new armchairs, glass in hand, eye on television, there was a knock at his door and there stood Delahaye, uninvited.

"I was just passing by," said Delahaye. "I just wanted to have a word with you about something. I'm not disturbing you, am I?" Delahaye's diminutive height and weight would normally preclude his hiding anything or anyone behind him, yet it indeed seemed that this time there was a presence at his back, in the shadows of the landing. Ferrer rose slightly on tiptoe. "Oh, right," said Delahaye, turning around, "excuse me. I'm with a friend. She's a bit shy. May we come in?"

There are, as anyone can tell you, people with botanical features. Some make you think of leaves, trees, or flowers: heliotrope, jonquil, baobab. As for Delahaye, always ill dressed, he called to mind those anonymous, grayish plants that grow in cities, between the exposed pavements of an abandoned warehouse yard, in the heart of a crack corrupting a ruined facade. Bony, atonal, discreet but tenacious, they know they have but a small role to play in life, but they know how to play it.

If Delahaye's anatomy, his behavior, his confused elocution evoked fearful weeds, then the friend who accompanied him fell under a different vegetal style. Christened Victoire and at first sight a beautiful but silent plant, she seemed more wild than ornamental or for pleasure, more datura than mimosa, not so much blooming as thorny, in short, not so easy to care for. Regardless, Ferrer knew right away that he would not lose sight of her. "Of course," he said, "come in." Then, lending only a distant ear to Delahaye's muddled statements, he did everything, as casually as you please, to make himself attractive to her and meet her gaze as often as possible. To little effect, at first glance; the battle seemed far from won, but who can ever say? Still, if told better, what Delahaye was relating that evening might not have been uninteresting.

On September 11, 1957, he explained, in Canada's extreme north, a small commercial vessel named the *Nechilik* had found itself stuck off the coast of the District of Mackenzie, at a place that remained undetermined to this day. As it was sailing between Cambridge Bay and Tuktoyaktuk, the *Nechilik* had been caught in an ice floe, carrying on board a load of fox, bear, and seal pelts, as well as a cargo of regional antiquities reputed to be extremely rare. Floundering after striking an uncharted rock, she was immediately engulfed by rapid-forming ice. The crew, who fled the paralyzed ship on foot at the cost of several frozen limbs, had had enormous trouble reaching the nearest base, where several of these limbs had to be amputated. In the following weeks, although the vessel's freight was of high commercial value, the region's isolation had dissuaded the Hudson Bay Company from trying to recover it.

Delahaye reported these facts, which he himself had just learned. He had even been led to understand that one could, if one looked hard enough, procure more detailed information regarding the exact coordinates of the *Nechilik*. There was of course some risk involved, but if more precise information could be had, the endeavor might prove highly worthwhile. Classically, there are four or five steps in the discovery of an ethnic or antique art object. Usually some pathetic local discovers the object; then there's the area big shot who oversees this kind of activity in the sector; then the middleman who specializes in that particular kind of art; then finally the gallery owner, followed by the collector, who form the last links in the chain. Each member of this little group, obviously, gets progressively richer, the object at least doubling in value at each step. Now, in the case of the *Nechilik*, if it were somehow possible to intervene directly, they could cut out all those middlemen by going on site themselves, thereby saving much time and money.

But that evening, to tell the truth, Ferrer had not paid too much attention to Delahaye's story, too preoccupied by Victoire, whom he never could have imagined would move into his place within a week. Had someone told him, he would have been delighted, though also no doubt a little concerned. But had someone also informed him that, of the three people gathered there that evening, each would disappear in one way or another before the end of the month, himself included, he would have been supremely concerned.

6

Normally, on the day they were due to cross the Arctic Circle, they would celebrate this passage. Ferrer was told of this allusively, in a mocking and vaguely intimidating tone colored with initiatory predestination. Still, he ignored the threat, assuming the ritual to be reserved for the Equator, for the tropics. Not so: such celebrations are also held in the cold.

That morning, then, three sailors disguised as succubi burst screaming into his cabin and blindfolded him, after which they dragged him in a forced march through a maze of passageways up to the gym, which had been draped in black for the occasion. They removed his blindfold: on a central throne sat Neptune in the presence of the commander and several lesser-ranking officers. Crown, toga, and trident, wearing diving fins, Neptune as played by the chief steward was flanked by the nail-biter in the role of Amphitrite. The water god, rolling his eyes, commanded Ferrer to prostrate himself, to repeat after him various idiocies, to measure the gym to the sixteenth of an inch, to retrieve a ring of keys with his teeth from a tub of ketchup, and other harmless pranks. All the time Ferrer was complying, it seemed to him that Neptune was quietly insulting Amphitrite. After which the commander delivered a little speech and handed Ferrer his certificate of passage.

That done, after the Arctic Circle had been crossed, they began to notice several icebergs. But only from afar: in general, ships prefer to avoid icebergs. Some were aimlessly scattered and others were in groups, immobile, in anchored armadas; some were smooth and glistening, all immaculate ice, while others were soiled, blackened, yellowed by moraine. Their outlines suggested animal or geometrical shapes, their sizes ranged from the Place Vendôme to the Champ-de-Mars. They nonetheless seemed more discreet, more worn-out than their Antarctic counterparts, which glided pensively in large tabular blocks. They were also more angular, asymmetrical, and ornate, as if they had twisted and turned several times in troubled sleep.

At night, when Ferrer, too, had trouble sleeping, he got up to pass his time on the bridge with the men on watch. The entire periphery of the bridge was glassed in, huge and empty like a waiting room at dawn. Under the sleepy supervision of an officer, two helmsmen swapped places every four hours before the consoles, sonar and radar, eyes riveted on the sight rule. Ferrer sat in a corner on the thick carpet. He looked at the fathomless landscape lit by powerful searchlights, even though when you got down to it there was nothing to see, nothing but infinite white in the blackness, so little to see that sometimes it was too much. To keep busy, he studied the charts, the GPS readings, and the weather faxes. Quickly initiated by the men on watch, he sometimes killed time by scanning all the radio frequencies: the whole thing took a good fifteen minutes, which was something, at least.

In the end, there was only one event worth noting, when for technical reasons they stopped in the middle of the ice floe. Since they had thrown over a ladder, on whose rungs the ice formed mountain profiles in miniature, Ferrer climbed down to have a look around. Infinite silence. No sound but that of his steps muffled by the snow and the exhalations of the wind, and once or twice the cry of a cormorant. Heading off a little way despite orders, Ferrer spotted a family of sleeping walruses, huddled against each other on a floating ice cube. Flanked by their companions, they were old monogamous walruses, bald and mustached, worn-out by fighting. Opening an eye now and again, a female fanned herself with the tips of her flippers before falling back asleep. Ferrer went back on board.

Then the usual course of things took over again, endlessly. There was nonetheless one way to combat boredom: slice up time like a sausage. Divide it into days (D minus 7, D minus 6, D minus 5 until arrival), but also into hours (I'm starting to get hungry: H minus 2 before lunch), into minutes (I've had my morning coffee: normally M minus 7 or 8 before hitting the toilet), and even into seconds (I take a spin around deck: approximately S minus 30; between the time spent deciding to take this spin and the time spent thinking about it afterward, I've gained a minute). In short, as in prison, you have to count, quantify the time for everything you do—meals, videos, crosswords or comic books—to nip boredom in the bud.

Although you could also do nothing at all, spend a morning reading on your bunk in the T-shirt and underwear from the night before, putting off washing and getting dressed. As the ice floe projects through the open hatchway a blinding, brutal whiteness that invades the entire cabin, the sinumbra effect leaving no room for even the slightest shadow, you hang a bath towel over the opening; you wait.

But there are a few distractions, even so, even if insignificant: the regular inspection of the cabins by the chief engineer and the security man, lifeboat and fire drills, drills in timed donning of the floatation survival suit with thermostat. You could also, as often as possible, visit nurse Brigitte; you could risk courting her a little when the radioman is at his post; you could compliment her on her abilities, her beautiful appearance, her tan that is so paradoxical in this climate. And so you could learn that, to combat depression or worse, a collective agreement prescribed that in areas without sun the female crew are allowed to enjoy ultraviolet rays four hours a week.

The rest of the time it's Sunday, a perpetual Sunday whose felt silence inserts a gap between sounds, things, even instants: the whiteness contracts space and the cold slows down time. It's enough to make you go numb in the amniotic warmth of the windowpane. You no longer even think of moving in that ankylosis; since crossing the Arctic Circle, you no longer set foot in the gymnasium. Basically, you just concentrate on mealtimes.

7

Pointed pupil on an electric green iris, like the eye on an old radio, cold smile but a smile all the same, Victoire had thus moved into Rue d'Amsterdam.

She had come without bringing much, just a small valise and a bag that she had left near the door, as if in a train station locker for an hour. And in the bathroom, apart from her toothbrush, a minuscule case contained three foldable accessories and three travel-size beauty products.

She remained there, spending most of her time reading in an armchair, facing the muted television. At first she spoke little, at least as little as possible for her, answering each question with another question. She always seemed on her guard, even when no outside threat justified it, though sometimes her distrustful air in fact threatened to inspire hostile ideas. When Ferrer had company, she always seemed to be one of the guests; he almost expected to see her leave at midnight with the others, but she stayed, she stayed.

Among the consequences of Victoire's presence at Ferrer's were more frequent visits from Delahaye, still as negligent as ever about his appearance. One evening when he showed up at Rue d'Amsterdam, even more shockingly dressed than usual—shapeless parka with sides flapping against green jogging pants—Ferrer decided to say something just as he was about to go, and pulled him aside for a moment on the landing: Don't take this the wrong way, Delahaye. He explained that it would be preferable for his associate to dress a little better when he was at the gallery, that an art dealer had to take care of his appearance. Delahaye looked at him uncomprehendingly.

"Put yourself in the collector's shoes," Ferrer had persisted in a low voice, again pressing the timer switch of the hall light. "He's come to buy a painting from you, this collector. He's hesitant. And you know what it means to him, buying a painting, you know how afraid he is of wasting his money, of missing his big chance, of passing up the next Van Gogh, of what his wife might say, all of that. He's so afraid that he doesn't even see the painting anymore, you see what I mean? The only thing he sees is you, the dealer, you in your dealer clothes. So it's *your* appearance that gets put in the picture, you get me? If you're wearing pauper's clothes, it's your poverty he'll put up there. Whereas if you're dressed impeccably, it's just the opposite, and so it's good for the painting, so that's good for everyone and especially for us. You see?"

"Yes," Delahaye said, "I think I see."

"Good," said Ferrer, "well, see you tomorrow."

"You think he understood?" he asked a moment later, without expecting a reply; but Victoire had already gone to bed. Turning off the lights one by one, Ferrer entered the dark room and, the following afternoon, he appeared at the gallery wearing a chestnut-colored tweed suit, striped shirt (navy on sky), knitted brown-and-gold tie. Having arrived earlier, the ill-shaven Delahaye was still wearing the same outfit, still more frayed than the night before—enough to make you think he'd slept in it, just look at that shirt!

"I think things are moving forward with the *Nechilik*," said Delahaye.

"The what?" said Ferrer.

"That boat," said Delahaye, "you know, the boat with the antiques. I think I've found some good informants."

"Oh, right," Ferrer said evasively, distracted by the bell at the entrance. "Look sharp," he hissed, "someone's here. Réparaz."

They know Réparaz. Réparaz is a regular. He earns enormous amounts of money in business, in which he gets enormously bored; it's just that it's not exhilarating every single day to have the world monopoly on Smartex. The only enjoyment he ever gets is when he comes to buy art. And he also likes being advised, told about the latest trends, brought around to meet the artists themselves. One Sunday when Ferrer took him to see the studio of an engraver near Porte de Montreuil, Réparaz, who never left the 7th arrondissement except to cross the Atlantic in his private jet, became positively giddy going through the 11th. Oh, what architecture, what an exotic population, incredible, I'd gladly do this with you every Sunday. Terrific. Had a great time, old Réparaz. But it didn't keep him from belonging to the hesitant category. At the moment, he was sniffing around a fairly expensive large yellow acrylic by Martinov, moving closer, standing back, moving closer again, etc. "Hang on," said Ferrer, still in a whisper, to Delahaye, "watch this. I'm going to give him the old downplay routine. They love it."

"So," he went, sidling up to the Martinov, "you like it?"

"There's something there," said Réparaz, "there's really something there. I find it, you know, how can I put it."

"I know, I see what you mean," said Ferrer. "But actually it's not very good. Frankly it's far from the best in the series (it's a series, by the way), and besides it's not entirely finished yet. Aside from the fact that, between you and me, Martinov is a bit pricey."

"Hmm. Really. Well," said the other, "personally I find that there's really something going on with that yellow."

"Of course," Ferrer conceded, "I'm not saying it's bad. But still, it is a little high-priced for what it is. If I were you, I'd have a look at this one instead," he continued, indicating a work composed of juxtaposed aluminum squares painted light green, hanging in a corner of the gallery. "Now this one is interesting. It's going to go fairly steep before long, but for now it's still quite reasonable. See how light it is? It's clear. Luminous."

"All the same, it's not much," said the captain of industry. "I mean, it doesn't really show you much."

"You might think so at first glance," said Ferrer.

"But at least when you come home and find that on your wall, you don't feel attacked. There's always that."

"Let me think about it," said Réparaz, leaving. "I'll be back with my wife."

"It's all good," Ferrer said to Delahaye, "you'll see. He's definitely going to buy the Martinov. You have to argue with them sometimes, give them the impression they're thinking for themselves. Hm, here comes another one."

Forty-eight years old, tuft of hair clinging to his lower lip, velvet jacket, a frame wrapped in brown paper under one arm, smiling broadly and named Gourdel, the "other one" was a painter whom Ferrer had represented for ten years. Bearing a canvas, he came to get news.

"It's not going too well," answered Ferrer in a weary voice. "You remember Baillenx, who bought one of your paintings? He brought it back, he doesn't want it anymore. I had to take it back. There was also Kurdjian, you remember him, who was thinking of buying something. Well, he's not thinking anymore, he'd rather buy an American. And then you have two big ones that were auctioned for practically nothing, so honestly it's not going well at all."

"Right," said Gourdel, who was smiling less broadly as he unwrapped the frame. "Well, I've brought you this."

"You have to realize it's partly your fault," Ferrer continued without even glancing at the object. "You screwed everything up when you decided to give up abstract and go representational on me. I had to change my whole strategy for your work. You know it causes a ton of problems when a painter changes all the time. People expect one thing, and then they get disappointed. You know as well as I do that everything gets labeled, it's easier for me to promote something that doesn't move around too much, otherwise it's a disaster. You know perfectly well how fragile all this is. You don't need me to tell you, you already know what I'm saying. Anyway, I can't take this one right now, I have to unload the others first."

A pause, then Gourdel hastily rewraps his frame, nods to Ferrer, and leaves. Outside he runs into Martinov, who's just heading in. Martinov is a young man with innocently cunning eyes; they exchange a few words.

"That asshole's trying to shove me in the closet," says Gourdel.

"I can't believe that," consoles Martinov. "He knows what you're doing, he has faith in you. He's got some artistic sense, after all."

"No," says Gourdel before heading off into the bland daylight, "nobody has any artistic sense anymore. The only ones who ever did were the popes and kings. Since then, nobody."

"So you saw Gourdel," said Ferrer.

"I just ran into him," said Martinov. "Things don't seem to be going too well."

"He's a complete wreck," said Ferrer. "Sales-wise he's not going anywhere at all, he's nothing more than a symbolic leftover. You, on the other hand, are doing just fine. Someone just came by a while ago, who's certainly going to take the large yellow. Apart from that, what are you working on these days?"

"Well, let's see," said Martinov. "I had my vertical series. I'm giving two or three of them to a group show."

"Hold on a minute," said Ferrer, "what's this about?"

"Nothing," said Martinov, "it's just for the Deposit and Consignment Building."

"What?" said Ferrer. "You're doing a group show at the Deposit and Consignment Building?"

"So what?" said Martinov. "What's wrong with the Deposit and Consignment Building?"

"Personally," said Ferrer, "I think it's ridiculous that you're showing at the Deposit and Consignment Building. Ridiculous. And a group show to boot. You're devaluing yourself. Take my word for it. Anyway, you can do as you please."

It was therefore in a fairly bad mood that Ferrer listened to all the general information that Delahaye had for him about Boreal art: the Ipiutak, Thule, Choris, Birnirk, and Denbigh schools; Paleoarctic cultures that succeeded each other between 2500 and 1000 B.C.E. When Delahaye began comparing materials, influences, and styles, Ferrer was less attentive than when he started talking numbers: indeed it seemed more and more likely that this abandoned shipwreck business, if it proved to be true, might be worth the trip. Now for the moment it hadn't proven to be anything, for lack of more precise information. But it was now in the last days of January and in any case, Delahaye reminded him, even if we knew more, weather conditions prevented them from leaving before spring, when, at those high latitudes, daylight breaks.

8

It was in fact just about to break when Ferrer opened an eye: the open hatchway sketched a pale gray-blue rectangle on one wall of his cabin. On the absurdly narrow bunk, it was not easy to turn over toward the opposite wall, and then, having managed it, Ferrer had no more than twelve inches of mattress on which to lie, but at least it was a lot warmer than on other mornings. He tried to firm up his position by slight movements, crawling in place on his side, if such a thing is possible: in vain. Then, as he was trying to increase these movements to gain a little of this warm territory, a sudden adverse force propelled him backward: Ferrer tumbled from his bunk. He fell with his full weight on his right shoulder, thought it was dislocated, and shivered: the cabin floor was all the colder in that Ferrer was nude except for his watch. He pulled himself up using all four limbs, then pondered the bunk while scratching his scalp.

It appears things had changed. The unforeseeable had happened. In the bunk, sighing with relief at being alone and turning over before starting to snore again, nurse Brigitte comfortably sank back into sleep. Her tan was deeper and more pronounced than usual, bistre fading to orange: she had fallen asleep again under the UV's, poor thing, and gotten a little overdone. Ferrer shrugged his shoulders, shivered again, and looked at his watch—six-twenty—before pulling on a sweater.

He wasn't feeling too well, to tell the truth, and was worried. The last time he went to see Feldman, the cardiologist had warned him against extremes of temperature: intense heat or intense cold, abrupt shifts in the weather: all of that was very bad for coronary cases. "You are not living a healthy life for someone in your condition," Feldman had said. "Quitting smoking isn't enough, you've got to follow a whole fitness program, every day, starting now." Ferrer had therefore been careful not to reveal that he was planning to leave for the Great North. He had just mentioned a business trip, in the vaguest of terms. "Good, and come back in three to four weeks," Feldman had said. "It'll be time to do an electrocardiogram, and I'll show you some good reasons to stop acting like an idiot." As he recalled these words, Ferrer mechanically placed a hand on his heart, just to make sure it wasn't beating too hard, too little, too irregularly: no, it was okay, it seemed to be doing fine.

He wasn't so cold now; he was quite a sight in his sweater, his poor contracted genitals barely swaying underneath. For lack of anything better to do, he cast a glance out the porthole. A distant glimmer gave some idea of the dawning sun that for the moment was reflected only by terns with immaculate wings spinning in the heights. In that dim light, Ferrer could barely make out to port the eroded mass of Southhampton Island fading behind them, grayish like an old heap of gravel: they were about to enter the channel leading into Wager Bay. Ferrer took off his sweater and got back into bed.

Not so easily done. Magnificently proportioned though she was, nurse Brigitte occupied the entire bunk: no room to slip in even an arm, no way to crawl in from the side. Bucking up his courage, Ferrer decided to approach the matter from above by lowering himself onto the nurse with all the delicacy he could muster. But Brigitte began to murmur disapprovingly. She balked and started to push him away, and for a moment Ferrer thought the battle lost, but little by little she relaxed. They got down to business, though with scant margin for error, the narrowness of the bunk prohibiting more combinations than it allowed: they could only manage one on top of the other, albeit alternatively and in both directions (which is already not bad). They took their time, given that it was Sunday; they indulged themselves, they lingered, and did not leave the cabin until ten o'clock that morning.

It was Sunday, a real Sunday. You could feel it in the air where several scattered squadrons of cormorants pushed forward more sluggishly than usual. Walking up the deck they met part of the crew coming from the chapel, among them the radiotelegraph operator who concealed his spite rather poorly. But in any case, they were about to reach Ferrer's goal; for the radioman it was only a matter of hours until he'd be forever rid of this rival who, having reached his objective, bid his farewells to the captain and staff on the bridge, then headed back to his cabin to pack his bags. The ice breaker dropped Ferrer in Wager Bay before immediately casting off again. That day a uniform fog hung over everything, expansive, opaque, low as a ceiling, masking the neighboring peaks and even the upper portion of the ship, but at the same time diffusing an extremely bright light. Once on land, Ferrer saw the *Des Groseilliers* disperse in the fog, its masses fade into outlines, then those outlines themselves fade into a mere sketch, which ended up evaporating as well.

Ferrer preferred not to linger in Wager Bay: it was nothing more than a group of prefab shacks with walls of rusted sheet metal pierced by little windows lit in dusty ochre. Between these buildings, which were huddled around a mast, several schematic roads barely breathed: narrow, uneven passageways warped by dirty ice, obstructed by snowdrifts, their intersections littered with dark masses of metal or cement and shreds of petrified plastic. Stiffly deployed like hung wash, albeit frozen horizontal, a flag flapped motionlessly at the top of the mast whose barely visible shadow stretched up to the cramped roundel of the heliport.

This small heliport was adjacent to a minuscule airport where Ferrer took off, heading for Port Radium, on board a Saab 340 Cityliner outfitted for six, even though the only passenger, apart from him, was an engineer from the Eureka weather station. Fifty minutes later, at Port Radium, which resembled Wager Bay like an unloved brother, Ferrer met his guides: two locals named Angoutretok and Napaseekadlak. They were dressed in quilted down with synchilla polar fibers, porous undergarments made of capilene, fluorescent snow suits, and gloves with a built-in heating system. Natives of the district next to Tuktoyaktuk, they were structurally identical, basically small and wide, with short legs and tapered hands, beardless pentagonal faces and sallow complexions, prominent cheekbones, stiff black hair, and dazzling teeth. Having first introduced themselves, they presented Ferrer to the sled dogs.

A pack dozing in a pen around a chief, these dogs were hairy, dirty, with yellowish-black or filthy-yellow pelts and surly dispositions. If they didn't much like the men who, not much liking them either, never petted them, they didn't even seem to care for each other very much: the looks they exchanged denoted only envy and jealousy. Ferrer quickly understood that, as individuals, not one of these animals was the sort you wanted to know. If you called one by name, he barely turned around, then turned away again if he didn't see any food. If you exhorted him to get to work, he didn't even react, signifying with a brief sideways glance that you should talk to the leader of the pack. The latter, aware of his importance, then made a face and gave a cursory acknowledgment with his eye—the annoyed eye of an executive under stress, the distracted eye of his secretary doing her nails.

They started out that same day: there they are, heading off. They were equipped with Savage 116 FFS All-Weather carbines, 15 × 45 IS binoculars with image stabilizers, knives, and whips. Napaseekadlak's knife had a handle made of oosik, the bone that acts as a walrus's sexual organ and whose qualities of suppleness, resistance, and porosity give it an ideal grip. Less traditional, Angoutretok's was a White Hunter II Puma with a Kraton handle.

Leaving Port Radium, they at first formed a small parade. On both sides, flecks of snowy ice were scattered on the rocks like a remainder of foam on the walls of an empty beer mug. They advanced fairly quickly, each one rudely jostled on his sled by the uneven ground. At first Ferrer tried to exchange a few words with his guides, especially Angoutretok, who spoke a little English; Napaseekadlak expressed himself only by smiles. But the words, once emitted, echoed too briefly before solidifying: as they remained frozen for an instant in the middle of the air, one had only to stretch out one's hand for these words to fall into it in a jumble, melt gently between one's fingers, and evaporate in a whisper.

Immediately the mosquitoes launched their attack, but fortunately they were easy to kill. In these latitudes, in fact, man is practically unknown to animals, who are not wary of him: you can kill mosquitoes with a backswipe of your hand, without them even trying to escape. Which didn't prevent them from making life unbearable, attacking by dozens per cubic yard and stinging through clothing, especially on the shoulders and knees where the fabric was taut. If the men had wanted to take a photo, the swarms, floating in front of the lens, would have blocked the view; but in any case they didn't have a camera, that wasn't what they were there for. Having covered the air holes of their hoods, they moved forward, batting at their sides.

Once they saw a polar bear, too far away to be a threat.

But it was mainly the dogs who caused all sorts of problems. One morning, for example, as Ferrer found himself ejected from his sled by a rugged snow ridge, the driverless vehicle began to careen every which way. But instead of stopping, the animals, thinking they were free, took off at top speed in several directions at once. The sled ended up spilling over and getting stuck across the trail, immobilizing at the end of their traces the dogs who immediately began yapping noisily at each other. Meanwhile, Ferrer tried to regain his senses on the edge of the trail while rubbing his hip. Having set the sled upright, Angoutretok tried to pacify the animals with his whip, but managed only to make things worse: instead of calming down, the first whipped dog reacted by biting his neighbor, who bit the one next to him, who bit two others, who reacted the same way until everything degenerated into total confusion. They were finally subdued with great effort; then the train headed off again. The boreal summer progressed. Night never fell.

9

In Paris, at the beginning of February, Ferrer might have been the first to disappear for good.

The end of the month of January had been very busy. After Delahaye had, insistently, revived the question of how interesting the *Nechilik* could be, Ferrer decided to take a serious look. Visiting museums and private collections, consulting experts, travelers, and curators, he began to learn firsthand all he could about polar art and its market value. If what remained of the ship should one day prove accessible, it would no doubt be an affair of consequence. Ferrer had even bought, from a gallery in the Marais, two small sculptures that he studied at length every evening: a sleeping woman by Povungnituk and a figuration of spirits by Pangnirtung. Although these forms were not familiar to him, he ended up trying to understand them, to distinguish their style, discern their intentions.

In any case, this northward operation remained hypothetical for the moment. Delahaye, despite his research, had still not turned up any information to help them locate the wreck more precisely. Already, however, in anticipation, Ferrer sketched the broad outlines of a possible expedition. But these winter days brought with them some new cares. Preparations for a first Martinov retrospective (after the latter had given up on

Deposits and Consignments), flood damage at Estrellas's studio (reducing all of his rock candy installations to nil), Gourdel's suicide attempt, and other preoccupations provoked an unusual heightening of activity. Without really noticing, Ferrer found himself buried under things to do, overworked like your average marketing manager. It was so unlike him that he didn't even realize how hard he was pushing himself. Several days later he would pay the price.

Several days, or rather nights, for soon afterward a physiological episode occurred: all of his exhausted vital functions fell asleep when he did. It lasted only two or three hours at most, during which time his biorhythms went on strike. The beating of his heart, the circulation of air in his lungs, perhaps even his cell regeneration worked only the barest minimum, hardly noticeable, a kind of coma, which uninitiates would have found almost impossible to distinguish from clinical death. Ferrer had no knowledge whatsoever of this episode taking place in his body, nor did he experience the slightest suffering. At most he passed through it as if in a dream, and perhaps he did indeed dream it—not a half-bad dream to boot, since he awoke in a pretty good mood.

He woke up later than usual and without realizing a thing. He didn't imagine for an instant that he'd just been victim to what is known as an atrioventricular block. Had he been examined, the specialists would no doubt have posited a Mobitz II block, before further reflection and consultation led them to settle on a diagnosis of second-degree Luciani-Wenckebach.

Whatever the case, when he awoke, Victoire wasn't there. Apparently she hadn't come home last night. Nothing so strange about that: the young lady sometimes spent the night at a girlfriend's, usually a certain Louise, or at least so she reassured him in her usual evasive, detached way—Ferrer not being exclusive or attached enough himself to seek further reassurance. Still, once out of bed, he first supposed that Victoire had changed rooms during the night to sleep in peace, for the simple reason that he snored, he knew he sometimes snored, no use denying it. And so he had gone to see whether Victoire was sleeping down the hall. No. Hm. Then, noting first that her toilet articles were missing from the bathroom, then her clothes from the closet, then she herself over the following days, there was no use denying either that she was gone.

As far as his time allowed, he looked for her the best he could. But if Victoire had any close friends he could ask for information, a little family, some next of kin or next best thing, she'd never introduced him to them. She had very few habits apart from three bars: the Cyclone, the Sun, and especially the Central, also frequented by Delahaye, but the latter was hard to reach these days, claiming to be occupied full-time with that *Nechilik* business. Two or three times, Ferrer had also seen Victoire in the company of the woman named Louise, who was the same age as she and had a part-time job at the train station. He revisited those bars, saw Louise, learned nothing.

And so once again he lives alone. But this isn't good for him. And still less so in the morning when he wakes up with an erection, in other words like most mornings like most men, while lurching between the bedroom, kitchen, and bathroom. Luckily, after these perambulations, it becomes no more than half an erection. But ballasted, almost unbalanced by that appendage perpendicular to the hunched vertical of his spine, he finally sits down, opens his mail—an almost always disappointing operation that generally and quickly ends in a new sedimentation of his wastepaper basket, but that, mutatis mutandis if not nolens volens, at least shrinks his apparatus back to normal size.

No, it isn't good for him; it can't last. But it's no mean feat to improvise when the void suddenly opens. Even Victoire's brief presence was long enough to erase other women's presences around Ferrer. He naively thought those others would always be there, as if, as potential stand-ins, they had nothing better to do than wait for him. But they all let him down, they haven't waited, of course; they're living their own lives. So, not being able to remain celibate for long, he goes looking where he can.

As everyone knows, you never find anyone when you're looking; it's better not to look like you're looking, act like nothing's happening. It's better to wait for some chance encounter, especially without looking like you're waiting, either. For so it is, they say, that great inventions are born: by the inadvertent contact of two products placed next to each other by chance on a laboratory table. Of course, this still requires someone to place these products next to each other, even if no one had planned their juxtaposition. It still requires someone to call them together at the same moment: proof that they had, well before anyone knew it, something between them. It's chemistry, and that's that. You can look far and wide for all kinds of molecules and try to combine them: nothing. You can have samples sent in from the four corners of the earth: still nothing. And then one day, by a slip of the hand, you jostle the objects that have been lying around on the tabletop for months, accidental splatter, test tube knocked over in a crystallizer, and immediately it produces the reaction you've been trying to get for years. Or, for example, you forget some cultures in a drawer and bingo: penicillin.

And indeed, following an analogous process, after long and vain searches during which Ferrer explored concentric circles further and further removed from Rue d'Amsterdam, he ended up finding what he'd been looking for in the person of his neighbor. Her name was Bérangère Eisenmann. Oddly enough, she really was the girl next door. Of course, let's not forget that such proximity is not purely advantageous. There is the good and the not-so-good, a problem that we would gladly try to explore in further detail if time allowed. But we cannot develop this point for the moment, since a more pressing bit of news demands our attention. Indeed, we've just learned of Delahaye's tragic disappearance.

10

The incidents with the dogs multiplied. Another day, for instance, between two transparent prisms of sharp ice, they came upon the body of a pachyderm that had been lying there since God knows when. Half buried, the corpse was sugared with ice, better preserved under the floe than a pharaoh in his pyramid: ice embalms just as thoroughly as it kills. Despite the guides' outbursts, curses, and whip cracks, the dogs swooped avidly down on the mastodon, and what ensued was only the panting, viscous, repugnant crackings of busy jaws. Then, once the animals were gorged, having gnawed down the exposed portion of the beast without even letting it thaw, the humans had to wait for the end of their siesta before getting back on the road. The humans were getting a little fed up with those dogs. This would be the last day they relied on their services. They continued to advance in the perpetual light ever more obscured by clouds of mosquitoes.

Let us recall that in this place, in this season, nothing separates the days: the sun never sets. You have to look at your watch to know when it's time to rest, to blindfold your eyes to sleep after dusting off the tent floor with a seagull's wing. As for the mosquitoes, their larvae having reached maturity in innumerable puddles, they attack all the harder. Now it's no longer by dozens but by hundreds per cubic yard that they lead their assaults in tight formation, entering your nose, mouth, ears, and eyes while you tread and trudge over the permafrost. On Angoutretok's advice, contrary to the prescriptions of the medical profession embodied by Feldman, Ferrer started smoking again, even though the rediscovered taste of tobacco, in this cold, made him gag. But it was the only way to repel the diptera: in their moments of fury, it was an even better idea to smoke two or three cigarettes in a row.

On they went, over a path they could barely make out, signposted every few miles with regularly erected cairns. Simple tumuli of stones piled up by the region's first explorers to mark their passage, the cairns had at first served as reference markers, but they could also contain objects bespeaking past activities in the area: old tools, calcified food remains, nonfunctioning weapons, and even, sometimes, printed or bone matter. Such as, once, a skull in whose eye sockets a little moss was growing.

And so they advanced, from cairn to cairn in lessening visibility, for the mosquitoes weren't the only ones darkening the environment: fog did its work as well. Not content with disturbing the air's transparency and thus removing objects from sight, fog could also enlarge them considerably. Unlike objects in a rearview mirror, which are always closer than they appear, sometimes in the white expanse they thought they were at arm's length from a cairn that was still an hour away by sled.

The pachyderm incident had finally outstripped the guides' patience. At the first station after Port Radium, at a Skidoo rental, they swapped all the dogs for three of the snowmobiles, to which they hitched light trailer sleds. They proceeded on these machines, which putt-putted away pathetically in the Arctic silence. Leaving numerous oil stains and greasy tracks behind them on the dusty ice, they continued to weave between the blocks, sometimes tracing long loops to skirt around the frozen barriers without ever meeting a single tree or the humblest blade of grass. It's only that things have changed quite a bit in the region, in the last fifty million years. Back then poplars grew here, and beech trees, vines and sequoias, but that's all finished now. Little more than yesterday, a bit to the south, you could occasionally spot some lichen, a vague briar, a weak birch, a crawling willow, a little Arctic poppy, an occasional mushroom; but these days, nothing, not the humblest vegetable as far as the eye can see.

They were still subsisting on the same individual rations, balanced, designed for this kind of enterprise. But in an attempt to improve on the standard fare, they once gathered a few angmagssaets, with an eye to a fry. After a huge block of glacier fell into the sea, a high wave had spilled those little sardine-sized fish onto the bank; more than anything they had to chase off the gulls who, threatening to dive-bomb, hovered silently above the catch. Another time, Napaseekadlak harpooned a seal. Now, it's well known that everything is usable in a seal; it's a little like the polar equivalent of pork: its flesh can be grilled, poached, simmered; its blood, which tastes like egg whites, makes a decent sausage; its fat provides light and heat; with its skin you can make excellent tent flaps; its bones yield needles and its tendons thread; and with its intestines you can even make lovely transparent curtains for the house. As for its soul, once the animal is dead, it rests in the tip of the harpoon. So Angoutretok prepared a dish of seal liver with canned mushrooms on the brazier, near which Napaseekadlak had laid his harpoon so the soul wouldn't catch cold. And while they ate, Angoutretok taught Ferrer several of the 150 words for snow in Iglulik, from crusty snow to squeaky snow to fresh soft snow, hard undulating snow, fine powdery snow, wet compact snow, and snow lifted by the wind.

The farther north they went the colder it got, as was to be expected. Icicles had clustered in perpetuity on all of Ferrer's facial hair: bangs and lashes, beard and brows, rim of the nostrils. He and his guides advanced behind their dark glasses past craters, cirques caused by meteorites, from which the locals, once upon a time, extracted iron to forge weapons. Once they spotted a second bear in the distance, alone on the ice, standing watch next to an air hole for seals. Too absorbed in his lookout, the polar bear ignored them, but just in case, Angoutretok acquainted Ferrer with the correct procedure to follow in event of an untimely encounter with a bear. Do not run away: the bear can run faster than you. Instead, try to distract him by tossing aside some colored piece of clothing. Finally, if a confrontation appears inevitable, remember as a last resort that polar bears are lefties: if you're stuck trying to defend yourself, might as well attack the animal from its weaker side. It'll probably do no good, but at least it's something.

There would be no funeral mass for Delahaye, just a late-morning benediction in a small church near Alésia. When Ferrer arrived, a fair number of people were already there, but he didn't recognize a single soul. He wouldn't have guessed that Delahaye had so many relatives or friends, but perhaps these were only resigned creditors. He discreetly took his place at the back of the church, neither in the very last row nor behind a pillar, but in the second-to-last row, not too far from a pillar.

Everyone had just entered, was about to enter, was entering: to avoid meeting gazes, Ferrer stared down at his feet, but his inner peace was short-lived: pushing through the crowd against the tide, a pale woman with sunken cheeks who wore a tailored damask suit came up to introduce herself: Delahaye's widow. Ah, said Ferrer, who hadn't known, who wouldn't have guessed either that the man had been married. Okay, fine, so he had been, well, gosh, so much the better for him.

Still, the widow informed him, she and Delahaye had not lived together for six years, had maintained separate residences, though in fact not too far from each other. For they had remained on good terms, called each other every three days, and each one had a key to the other's apartment to look after the plants and the mail when the other was away. But after a week, worried about Delahaye's silence, she had finally gone into his home to discover his lifeless body on the tiled floor of the bathroom. "That's the whole problem with living alone," she concluded with an interrogative look.

"Of course," agreed Ferrer.

Then the widow Delahaye, who had, she said, heard a lot about him, Louis-Philippe liked you very much, imperatively suggested that Ferrer sit beside her in the front pew.

"Gladly," he lied, rising against his will. Still, he rationalized, since this was basically the first time he'd attended such a ceremony, at least it would be a chance to see more or less how it went.

In fact, it was fairly simple. You've got a coffin on a trestle, placed feet forward. At the base of the coffin you've got a wreath of flowers in the occupant's name. You've got a priest who concentrates on backstage left and an attendant at the front of stage right—ruddy corpulence of a psychiatric nurse, dissuasive expression and black suit, an aspergillum in his right hand. You've got people who have just sat down. And when the nearly full church falls silent, the priest intones a few prayers, followed by an homage to the dearly departed, then he invites the audience to kneel before the remains or bless them with the aspergillum, as they choose. It's fairly quick and then it's over. Ferrer is getting ready to watch the audience kneel when the widow pinches his arm, indicating the coffin with her chin and raising her eyebrows. As Ferrer knits his own in incomprehension, the widow raises and indicates more forcefully while pinching him tighter and giving him a shove. It seems it's his turn to act. Ferrer stands up; the audience watches; Ferrer is mortified but he steps forward. He doesn't quite know what to do, never having done it.

The attendant hands him the aspergillum and Ferrer takes it without being sure he's holding it right side up, then begins to shake it haphazardly. Without meaning to trace any particular figures in the air, he nonetheless forms several circles and bars, a triangle, a St. Andrew's cross, walking in a circle all around the coffin before the public's astonished eyes, without knowing when or how to stop until the audience starts to murmur and, soberly but firmly, the attendant anchors him by one sleeve to repatriate him in his front-row seat. But in that instant, surprised by the attendant's grip and still brandishing the aspergillum, Ferrer lets go of the object: it flies against the coffin, which produces a hollow thud under the shock.

Later, leaving the church with a troubled mind, Ferrer spotted the widow Delahaye in conversation with a young woman: it took him a few seconds to recognize Louise. They turned toward him once while still talking; their expressions changed the moment they noticed he was watching. Deciding to approach them, Ferrer had to ford a passage through the audience members loitering in small groups as if around a theater exit, who turned as he went by just as if they had recognized the actor from the aspergillum scene.

Before Ferrer could ask anything, Louise reiterated

that she still had no news of Victoire. The widow, without having been asked either, insisted that Delahaye's disappearance created a void that nothing could ever fill. To the point that, she stated with exaltation, it seemed unthinkable that Delahaye should not continue postmortem to make his presence felt. In the meantime, they would reconvene at the cemetery at tea time. Thus summoned, Ferrer could not beat a quiet retreat. But it's a fact that, postmortem, as he was returning home on Rue d'Amsterdam before going out again for the burial, a large, tan, unpostmarked envelope, slipped under his door well past the mailman's hour of passage, increased the trouble in his mind. Bearing his name and address printed in an anonymous hand, the envelope contained the coordinates of the *Nechilik*.

At 118° east longitude and 69° north latitude, more than sixty miles past the arctic polar circle and fewer than six hundred from the magnetic North Pole, the wreck had come to rest in Amundsen Gulf, at the northernmost limit of the Northwest Territories. The closest town was called Port Radium. Ferrer consulted his atlas.

The poles, as anyone can testify, are the most difficult region in the world to study on a map. You never quite get satisfaction. It could be one of two things: you can consider the poles as occupying the top and bottom of a classic planisphere, with the Equator acting as the median horizontal base. But then it's as if you were looking at them in profile, in vanishing perspective and always necessarily incomplete—it doesn't really do the trick. Or else you can study them from above, as if from an airplane: such maps exist. But in that case, it's their articulation with the continents, which you normally see head-on, so to speak, that are suddenly missing, and that's no good either. Poles, therefore, do not make very good flat spaces. Forcing you to think in several dimensions at once, they pose multiple problems to the cartographic mind. The best thing would be to use a globe, but Ferrer has none. Still, he manages to get some idea of the place: very far, very white, very cold. That done, it's time to head for the cemetery. Ferrer leaves his apartment and what do you think greets him? His next-door neighbor's perfume.

Bérangère Eisenmann is a big-boned, fun-loving girl, highly perfumed, really quite fun-loving and really way too perfumed. When Ferrer finally noticed her, the deal was done within a few hours. She had come by his place for a drink, then they went out to dinner. She said, Should I leave my bag? He said, Sure, leave your bag. Then, after the first rush of excitement, Ferrer had started to get suspicious: women who are too close pose problems, and all the more so next-door neighbors. Not that they were too available, which would be fine, but that he, Ferrer, became too available to them, possibly against his will. Of course, you never get without giving; of course, you have to know what it is you want.

But most of all, the perfume issue quickly became a problem. Extatics Elixir is a terribly sour and insistent scent, which teeters dangerously on the cusp between spikenard and cesspit, which satisfies while it attacks, excites while it smothers. Every time Bérangère came over, Ferrer would have to wash thoroughly afterward—a remedy that was only moderately effective, so much had the perfume seemingly insinuated itself under his skin. So he changed the sheets and towels, threw his clothes directly into the washer, rather than in the hamper where they would have definitively contaminated all the others in short order. Try as he might to air out the apartment, the odor took hours to dissipate, and moreover it never faded away entirely. It was so powerful that all Bérangère had to do was call and, carried by the telephone wires, her scent would infest the apartment anew.

Before meeting Bérangère Eisenmann, Ferrer knew nothing about Extatics Elixir. Now he can still smell it as he creeps toward the elevator on tiptoe: the perfume seeps through the keyhole, the gaps in the doorframe, follows him into his own home. Of course he could suggest that Bérangère change brands, but he doesn't dare. Or he could buy her another, but various arguments dissuade him, it might seem like too much of a commitment, oh for God's sake, get me to the North Pole.

But we're not there yet. First we have to go to the Auteuil cemetery, a small parallelepiped of a graveyard, bordered to the west by a high wall and to the north, along Rue Claude-Lorrain, by an office building. The two other sides are lined by apartment houses whose windows, looking out on the interlaced network of paths, enjoy an unimpeded view of the tombstones. These are not luxury apartments such as normally flourish in these rich neighborhoods, but rather low-income units upgraded with new windows from which, in the graveyard silence, various scraps of noise drift down like scarves: kitchen or bathroom sounds, shouts from radio game shows, fights and screaming children.

An hour before the participants arrived, fewer in number than at the Alésia church, a man appeared before the concierge of one of these buildings, via the entrance on Rue Michel-Ange. The man stood very straight, spoke with economy; his face was inexpressive and almost frozen, and he was wearing a new-looking gray suit.

"I've come about the studio for rent on the sixth floor," he said. "I called on Monday to see it."

"Oh, right," the concierge remembered. "Baumgarten, wasn't it?"

"Tner," the man corrected. "Baumgartner. May I have a look? Don't trouble yourself, I'll just run up a moment and let you know if I like it." The concierge handed him the keys to the studio.

The aforementioned Baumgartner entered the studio, which was fairly dark because of its northern exposure. It was carpeted in tan and furnished sparsely with dark-colored and depressing objects, such as a brown-striped bench soiled with dubious substances and continental stains, a chipped Formica table, curtains stiff with greasy dust, and sticky dark-green drapes. But the newcomer crossed the studio without looking around and headed toward the window, which he opened only a crack, standing slightly back from it and to one side, invisible from the exterior as he was partly hidden behind one of the drapes. From there, he followed the entire burial ceremony with great attention. Then he went back down to see the concierge and told her no, it wasn't really what he was looking for, a bit dark and too damp, and the concierge admitted that, indeed, it wouldn't hurt to give the place a touch-up.

It was too bad, Baumgartner continued, because it was precisely this neighborhood he was interested in, but someone had told him about something else not too far away, and the concierge, not one to hold a grudge, wished him good luck as he went off to see that something else, at the top of Boulevard Exelmans. In any case, Baumgartner would never have taken the studio on Michel-Ange.

12

They spotted the *Nechilik* one fine morning, still a fair distance away: a small tapering mass the color of soot and rust sitting on an ice floe punctuated by rocky outcroppings, an old broken toy on a ragged sheet. It appeared to be stuck in the ice at the foot of an eroded knoll, which was partly covered with snow but with one flank breaking into a succession of brief, bare cliffs. At that distance, the wreck appeared fairly well preserved: maintained by the still-taut shrouds, its two small, intact masts stood patiently, and the pilot house in the after part of the vessel still appeared solid enough to shelter a few shivering specters. Knowing that these regions were rich in hallucinations, more-over, and at first suspecting the boat itself to be but a phantom, Ferrer waited until he was fairly close up before fully believing in its reality.

Illusion indeed reigns under these skies. Only yes-terday they were pushing forward behind dark glasses, without which the arctic sun fills your eyes with sand and your head with dead weight, when this same sun was suddenly multiplied in the frozen clouds by par-helia: Ferrer and his guides had been blinded by five simultaneous suns aligned horizontally, one of which was the real thing—with two further stars perpendicular to the real thing. It lasted a good hour before the actual sun found itself alone once more.

The moment they saw the wreck, Ferrer signaled to his guides to be quiet and slow down as if it were a living creature, a potentially hostile polar bear. They cut the speed on the Skidoos, choked their motors before approaching cautiously, with the gait of land-mine specialists, pushing their vehicles by the handle-bars before leaning them against the ship's steel hull. Then, while the two locals kept their distance from the *Nechilik*, pondering the object gravely, Ferrer went to board it alone.

It was, then, a small merchant vessel, eighty feet long, on which a copper plate, riveted to the base of the rudder, stated its date of construction (1942) and place of registration (Saint John, New Brunswick). The body of the ship and its rigging seemed to be in good shape, dusted with frost and looking brittle as dead wood. What must once have been two crumpled pieces of paper flitting around deck amid the knots of ropes had become two sand roses on a background of cryo-genized snakes, the whole thing preserved under a layer of ice that did not soften even under Ferrer's boots. The latter entered the pilot house and gave it a once-over: an open log book, an empty bottle, a spent rifle, a calendar from the year 1957 decorated with a rather underdressed girl who brutally evoked and ex-acerbated the ambient temperature, which was −10°. The freeze-dried pages of the log prevented anyone from leafing through it. Through the cabin windows, on which no gaze had fallen in more than forty years,

Ferrer glanced out at the white landscape. Then, climbing down into the hold, he immediately found what he was looking for.

Everything seemed to be right there, as expected, squeezed into three fat metal trunks that had honorably resisted the climate. Ferrer had some difficulty loosening the lids welded shut by the cold, then, having given their contents a cursory check, he climbed back up on deck to call his guides. Angoutretok and Napaseekadlak went to join him with circumspection, reverently and not without hesitation, moving around the body of the ship as if they had illegally entered an isolated vacation home. The trunks were heavy and the iron stair leading down to the hold supernaturally slick; it was quite an ordeal to hoist them up on deck before unloading them. They attached their cargo the best they could to the trailer sleds, then caught their breath. Ferrer said nothing; the two guides giggled between themselves and swapped untranslatable jokes. The whole thing seemed to leave them basically cold, whereas he, Ferrer, was pretty moved by it all. There. It's done. Nothing left but to go home. But they could have a little something to eat, maybe, before starting up, suggested Napaseekadlak.

While the latter, in charge of lighting the fire, chopped away with his hatchet at the *Nechilik*'s mizzen mast, Ferrer, followed by Angoutretok, went back down to inspect the hold in greater detail. The few pelts that had been part of the cargo were still there as well, but unlike the rest they were not so well preserved, hard as tropical wood and with almost all the hairs fallen from the skin: no doubt they had lost pretty much all their commercial value. Ferrer nonetheless picked out a small white fox that seemed to have held up a bit better than the others and that he would thaw out to give, but to whom? We'll see. In what appeared to have been the galley, he had to dissuade Angoutre-tok from opening a can of monkey meat expired nearly half a century ago. Sure, it was a shame not to be able to take the few nifty things still on board the *Nechilik*, pretty little copper lamps, for example, an elegantly bound Bible, a superb sextant. But they were weighted down enough as it was for the return trip, and they could not afford any excess baggage. Later, after they had eaten, it was time to head back.

Slowed down by the weight, it took them a long time to reach Port Radium. Like a switchblade that flips open without warning, small shafts of steely wind sometimes rose to cut their momentum, slow their pace, and the polar spring opened unexpected breaches in the permafrost: once Ferrer fell in to mid-thigh; then it was a whole ordeal to pull him back out and dry him off, warm him up. They spoke still less than on the trip out, ate quickly, slept lightly. Ferrer, in any case, thought only of his booty. At Port Radium, through second cousins, Angoutretok found him a room with a cement floor in a kind of club or activity center, which was the closest thing around to a hotel. Finally, alone in his room, Ferrer opened the crates and took stock of their contents.

As anticipated, they were indeed filled with exceed-ingly rare Paleoarctic art, falling into the various styles that Delahaye and other experts had introduced him to. There were, among other things, two sculpted mammoth tusks covered with blue vivianite, six pairs of snow goggles made from reindeer antlers, a small whale carved in baleen, an ivory corset with laces, a device for putting out caribou eyes made from broken caribou bone, inscribed tablets, quartz dolls, knick-knacks made of seal ulna and musk-ox horn, engraved narwhal and sharks' teeth, rings and stamps forged from meteorite nickel. There were also a fair number of magical or funerary objects shaped like pretzels or sprockets, made of soapstone or polished nephrite, red jasper, green slate, and flint in blue, gray, black, and every color of serpentine. Then masks of all kinds and, to top it off, a collection of skulls with their mouths plugged by obsidian rails, their eye sockets obstructed by balls of walrus ivory encrusted with onyx pupils. A fortune.

1 3

Let us shift horizons for a moment, if you will, to rejoin the man who answers to the name of Baumgartner. Today, Friday, June 22, while Ferrer is trudging over the ice floe, Baumgartner is wearing a checkered suit of anthracite-colored virgin wool, slate-gray shirt, and iron-gray tie. Although summer has officially just arrived, the sky matches his outfit, basely expectorating a brief, intermittent spittle. Baumgartner is walking up Rue de Suez, served by the metro stop Château-Rouge, in Paris's 18th arrondissement. It's one of those small streets off Boulevard Barbès festooned with African butcher shops, live fowl purveyors, parabolic antennas, and joyful polychromatic fabrics of the bazin, batik, and java varieties, printed in the Netherlands.

On the even-numbered side of Rue de Suez, most of the doors and windows of the depressing old buildings are blinded by roughly mortared concrete blocks, the sign of expropriation or impending annihilation. One of these is not entirely obstructed: two windows on the top floor still breathe, though faintly. Protecting faded curtains, their panes are matte with dust—one of them cracked diagonally and reinforced with packing tape, the other, missing, replaced by a framed black trash bag. Stuck in mid-swing, the building's entrance door at first looks onto two mismatched rows of anonymous, disemboweled mailboxes, then on a staircase with uneven steps and hugely fissured walls. Here and there, courtesy of the city's public works department, references flanked by handwritten dates bear witness to the implacable progress of these fissures. Since the light switch is out of order, Baumgartner gropes his way blindly to the top floor. He knocks on a door, is about to push it open without waiting for an answer when it seems to fly open by itself and a tall, gaunt fellow of about thirty rushes past Baumgartner, practically knocking him over. In the darkness, Baumgartner can barely make the man out: long face and balding forehead, nasty smile and aquiline nose, mitts tapered in curlicues, taciturn and no doubt with good night vision, since he charges surefootedly down the black stairway.

Opening the door, Baumgartner knows he won't want to close it again behind him. And in fact, the stifling funk-hole he enters does not inspire a sense of well-being; it's a kind of interior wasteland, a wasteland turned inside out like a glove. While it is bounded by four walls and protected by a ceiling, the floor is indistinguishable under the garbage, wrappings of expired foodstuffs, heaps of ratty togs, shredded magazines and moldy flyers made all but unreadable by the slop of a candle, planted in a can set on a crate. Overheated by a butane burner, the air is no more than a block of odors, part stuffiness, part mildew, and part burnt gas. It's hard to breathe. A radio-cassette player, at the foot of a mattress, broadcasts something indistinct at low volume.

The features of the young man stretched out on the purulent foam mattress, in a knot of blankets and deflated cushions, are not too distinct either. Baumgartner comes nearer, and this young man with his closed eyes does not look very fresh. He might even look a little bit dead. The radio-cassette player acts as a stand for a small spoon and a hypodermic needle, a scrap of dirty cotton wool, and the remains of a lemon. Baumgartner immediately gets the picture, but he's worried all the same.

"Hey, Flounder," he says, "hey. Flounder."

As he bends over, he sees that The Flounder is breathing. It looks like a mild case of discomfort, or else too much comfort. In any case, even closer up, even adding a candle, whatever the distance and the light, The Flounder's physiognomy remains ill-defined, as if Nature had exempted him of a specific appearance. He's a pale, charmless person, wearing dark clothes that have no charm either; still, he doesn't seem excessively dirty. Besides, he's opening one eye.

He's even rising wearily onto his left forearm and stretching out a hand to Baumgartner, who pulls back his own as soon as possible from those tepid and slightly oily fingers; who recoils and, his eyes casting about for a seat, notices only a wobbly bench. He gives up and remains standing. The other falls back on his support, complaining of nausea. "What I need," he says in a slow-motion voice, "is some tea. Maybe. But on the other hand, I really don't feel like getting up. I really really don't."

Baumgartner makes a face but it seems he can't really refuse; apparently he needs to have the other regain his senses. Making out an abstract kettle sitting next to an obscure sink, he fills it and places it on a butane stove, then unearths from the bottom of the wasteland a cup without a handle and a cracked bowl. These receptacles are disproportionate. The man called The Flounder, his eyes closed again, now alternately smiles and grimaces. While waiting for the water to boil, Baumgartner searches in vain for some sugar, fishes out some leftover lemon rinds for lack of anything better. The radio continues to kill time. "So," says The Flounder when he's drunk his tea, "when do we start?"

"A matter of days," answers Baumgartner, pulling a cell phone from his pocket. "It should be over and done by the end of this month. The thing is, from now on I have to be able to reach you at all times," he says, holding the phone out to the young man. "You'll have to be ready the moment the stuff shows up."

The Flounder snatches the phone away, simultaneously exploring his left nostril with his index finger, then, having examined in turn the phone and his finger: "Cool," he concludes from his examination. "What's the number?"

"Forget about the number," says Baumgartner. "I'm the only one who knows it, and that's how I like it. I should tell you one thing about this phone right away. It's not set to make outgoing calls, okay? It only receives. Its only use is for *you* to listen to *me* when I call *you*, you got that?"

"Fine," says the young man, now blowing his nose into his sleeve.

"So naturally you keep it on you at all times," says Baumgartner, refilling the receptacles.

"Naturally," says The Flounder. "The thing is, though, I might need a little something up front."

"Of course," allows Baumgartner, digging in his pocket for six five-hundred-franc bills folded in a paper clip.

"Great," comments The Flounder, handing back the paper clip. "Though a little more would be even better."

"No way," says Baumgartner, nodding toward the equipment lying on the radio. "I know you, you'll blow it all on that shit." During the negotiations that follow, at the close of which he ends up shelling out four more bills, Baumgartner mechanically unbends the paper clip until he obtains a more or less rectilinear stem.

Later, in the street, Baumgartner verifies that no residual filth, no miserable molecule floating in the air at The Flounder's has landed on his clothes. Still, he brushes them off as if the polluted ambience alone had contaminated them, even though he had been careful not to come into contact with anything; he'd just have to wash his hands and maybe brush his teeth when he gets home. Meanwhile, he walks back to the Château-Rouge station to return to his new domicile. It's still an off-peak hour and the metro is only half full: a number of bench seats are available, but Baumgartner opts for a fold-down seat on the aisle.

I'm Gone

In the metro, whatever the train's fullness coefficient, and even when it's empty, Baumgartner always prefers fold-down seats to the main benches, unlike Ferrer who prefers the latter. On the benches, which face each other in pairs, Baumgartner would unavoidably be exposed to sitting next to or opposite someone, most often both at the same time. Which would lead to still more frictions and inconveniences, contacts, difficulties in crossing or uncrossing his legs, parasitic glances, and conversations about which he couldn't care less. All things considered, even in rush hour when you have to stand up to make room, the fold-down seat strikes him as superior in every way. It is individual, mobile, and of flexible use. It goes without saying that the all-too-rare single fold-down seat is to his mind better still than the paired fold-down seat, which presents its own share of promiscuous inconveniences— the latter, in any case, less egregious than the nuisances of the bench. That's just how Baumgartner is.

Half an hour later, back in his new lodgings on Boulevard Exelmans, discovering the small bit of iron wire between his fingers, Baumgartner simply cannot bring himself to throw it out. He plants it in a pot of flowers and goes to lie down on the sofa. He's just going to rest his eyes for a moment. He'd love to take a nap, get away from all this for twenty minutes, maybe even a half hour if that's all right, but no, not a chance.

14

Ferrer had not slept a wink that night either, of course. Kneeling before the open trunks, he had turned each of the objects in all directions at least a thousand times. By now he was exhausted, no longer had the strength to look at them, no longer knew what he was seeing, lacked even the energy to be happy. Riddled with aches and pains, he got up with groans of protest, walked to the window and saw that the sun was already rising. But no, his mistake, in Port Radium the sun had not slept any more than he had.

Ferrer's room looked like a small one-person dormitory, which seems like a contradiction in terms and yet it's so: blank, characterless walls, lightbulb dangling from the ceiling, linoleum floor, cracked sink in one corner, bunk beds of which Ferrer chose the lower, out-of-order TV, closet containing only a deck of cards—auspicious at first, but in fact unusable because it was missing the ace of hearts—strong odor of frying pan and gurgling heater. Nothing to read but in any case Ferrer didn't much feel like reading, and finally he managed to sleep.

After the visit to the *Nechilik*, they were catching their breath in Port Radium. Each time they caught it, moreover, a torrent of spiraling steam, dense as cotton wool, escaped from their lips before crashing against the frozen marble of the air. Once Angoutretok and Napaseekadlak were thanked, paid, and heading back to Tuktoyaktuk, Ferrer had to remain for two solid weeks in this town, where the hotel choices came down to his room, which was next to a laundromat. Whether the building was a club, an annex to something, or an activity center, Ferrer would never know for sure, given that it was always empty and the manager mute. Or in any case not very chatty, for perhaps at heart he was suspicious, so rare were tourists in those god- and manforsaken holes: the days are endless, the distractions nonexistent, and the weather stinks. Given that there's no police station or representative of any authority whatsoever, one might suspect the resident stranger of fleeing some form of justice. A fair number of days and dollars, smiles and sign language were required for Ferrer to finally take the edge off the manager's circumspection.

Nor was it easy to find, among the populace of Port Radium, an artisan capable of making containers suited to the *Nechilik*'s cargo. All the more difficult in that wood practically doesn't exist in these climates: you don't find any more of that than of anything else, but as always anything is possible if you're willing to pay the price. Ferrer met the manager of the supermarket who agreed to adapt to the desired size some solid television, refrigerator, and machine-tool crates. It would take a while, and Ferrer had to wait. Usually keeping to his room since he didn't like to leave his antiques; getting bored rigid when he couldn't stand to look at them anymore. Port Radium can really be a drag, nothing much happening here, especially on Sunday when tedium, silence, and the cold worked together at peak efficiency.

He occasionally went out for a walk, but there wasn't much of anything to see, either: three times more dogs than people and twenty little houses in mellow colors, with tin roofs, along with two lines of buildings fronting the port. In any case, given the temperature, Ferrer never stayed out for long. Through the almost empty streets he took a quick stroll around these houses built with rounded corners to keep the cold from catching in the angles, to leave the least possible hold for ice. Heading toward the dock, he skirted the yellow clinic, the green post office, the red supermarket, and the blue garage, in front of which stood rows of Skidoos. At the port, other rows of boats on drydock awaited a more clement season. Most of the snow on the ground had melted but the ice floe, pierced only by a narrow channel, still obstructed a large portion of the bay.

In the general calm, he observed some occasional activity. Two provident individuals, taking advantage of the thaw, were digging holes in the momentarily movable earth with an eye toward burying those of their loved ones who would die in the coming winter. Two others, surrounded by prefabricated materials, were assembling their house kit, carefully following the instructions with the help of an explanatory video; smashing the silence, a generator powered the VCR in the open air. Three children were bringing empties back to the supermarket. Near the port, an old metal

church overlooked the shore where two iron-gray Zo-
diacs, having forged a passage in the channel, unloaded
in hiccups twelve passengers wearing anoraks and
large shoes. The lake's frozen lid had begun to come
undone in huge plates with simple outlines, like pieces
of an elementary jigsaw puzzle for beginners, and, beyond that, streaming under the pale sun, a hundred or
so large and small icebergs waddled along. Heading
back to his lodging, Ferrer again came across the two
men building their house. No doubt to take their mind
off things, to take a break, they had swapped the build-
er's video for another of pornographic character, which
they pondered gravely, standing, immobile and medi-
tative, without a word.

For the first several days, Ferrer took his meals alone
in his room and did not try to communicate with anyone except the manager. But the manager's conversation, even after he seemed to be reassured, was not all
that scintillating. Besides, talking only in gestures gets
tiresome. During his brief excursions, the few locals he
met always smiled at him, and Ferrer smiled back, but
that's as far as it went. Then, two days before his departure, as he was trying to peer through a yellowed
window at the inside of a house, he saw a young girl in
the background who smiled at him like the others. He
smiled back, but this time the girl's parents joined in.
Jovial, apparently having nothing better to do, they
invited him inside for a drink. To chill the whiskey,
they sent the girl to chip some ice off the nearest
ice floe, then they drank hard while chatting in broken
English; soon they insisted he stay for dinner, seal

mousse and baby whale steaks. But first they showed him around the house: well insulated, telephone and television, large stove and modern kitchen, cheap white-wood furniture of the Nordic variety, which can be found almost anywhere, even in the outskirts of Paris.

So Ferrer fraternized with the entire Aputiarjuk family. At dinner, he had some difficulty making out the father's profession before he understood that the latter had none. The recipient of unemployment benefits, he preferred to hunt for seal in the great outdoors rather than sweat in some tiny office, large kitchen, or huge ship. Even fishing, in this man's eyes, was just a horrid livelihood: nothing like seal hunting, the only true sport that gives you any real pleasure. Ferrer gave a little toast like the others. They drank copiously to seal hunting, affectionately to the health of seal hunters, enthusiastically to the health of seals in general, and soon, succumbing to the alcohol, they invited him to spend the night if he wanted; no problem with sharing the girl's room and in the morning they would tell each other their dreams as was customary in these parts, in every family, every morning. Ferrer found it hard to refuse; the lamp shed a soft glow and the radio was playing Tony Bennett, it was warm, the stove rumbled, everyone was laughing, the girl was smiling at him, ah, let's hear it for Port Radium.

15

So after his visit to The Flounder the other day, it was on a fold-down subway seat that Baumgartner returned to his new address; then a good week went by. This apartment is located not far from Rue Michel-Ange, behind a gateway cast off from Boulevard Exelmans: three 1930s villas are scattered there smack in the middle of a large garden, at the back of the Vietnamese embassy.

Now, you can't imagine how pretty the 16th arrondissement can be seen from inside. You probably imagine that it's as sad and gray as it appears at first glance, but you're very wrong. Conceived as ramparts or masks, these austere boulevards and mortiferous streets only look sinister: actually, they conceal houses that are remarkably welcoming. It's just that one of the most ingenious ruses devised by the rich consists in making you believe that they're bored in their neighborhoods, so much so that you might even begin to pity them, feel sorry for them, and commiserate over their fortune as if it were a curse carrying with it an inescapably depressing lifestyle. Yeah, sure. Forget about it.

At the top floor of one of those villas, Baumgartner is renting a very large studio for a very large sum of money. The stairway leading to it is dark green, almost black. As for the studio itself, its walls are made of brown marble, the fireplace of white-veined marble, and spotlights are embedded in the ceiling. Long, practically empty shelves, long table with a dirty plate on it, long sofa draped in a blue slipcover. The room is vast enough for a huge Bechstein piano pushed into a corner to be a mere detail, for the giant television lodged in another corner to look like a minuscule porthole. No other unnecessary furniture: only a gargantuan closet housing a considerable wardrobe composed of new-looking clothes. Tall windows are prolonged by a balcony bordered by a narrow, hollowed-out guardrail, full of earth that hosts the spiritless growth of weeds and other plant life, including a dandelion.

In the few days he has lived there, Baumgartner has gone out as little as possible. He runs few errands and orders his food by phone for delivery. Removed from the world, he seems to be awaiting his final hour. He does almost nothing all day long. He tips the delivery boys generously. Organized like a bachelor, he apparently knows how to fend for himself. Still, he is not a bachelor. The proof is that he's calling his wife.

The cordless device lets him move around the studio as he talks. "Yes," he says while passing from the Bechstein to the window, "I mean, you know what it's like when you're alone. Mostly frozen dinners," he specifies while manipulating the TV remote, muting the sound and flipping through the channels: sitcoms, documentaries, game shows. "No," he says, "I forgot the vitamins, you're right. In any case," he nuances without finishing his sentence, turning off the image to look out the window: clouds, morning glories, magpies.

"Fine, but I haven't seen any drugstores around here. In any case," he resumes, walking to the Bechstein, sitting down at it and adjusting the bench to his height. Pressing the mute pedal, he plants on the keyboard the only third chord he knows. "Oh, yeah, you heard that, did you? No, it's a baby grand. Anyway, listen, it would be good if you could find out as soon as he gets back," he says, standing up, moving away from the piano. As he walks by a flowerpot, he pulls out the little metal wire that he stuck in there the other day: he wipes off the dirt and twists it into the shape of several things: spiral, lightning bolt, television antenna.

"How the hell should I know!" Baumgartner suddenly explodes. "Make eyes at him or something. Stop, yes, right, of course you know," he smiles while massaging the wings of his nose. "But I think it would be better for me to get away for a bit. I don't want to risk running into anyone. I'm keeping the studio but I'm going to spend a few days in the country. Of course I'll let you know. No, I'm leaving this evening, I prefer driving at night. Naturally. Of course not. Yeah, love you too."

He hangs up, then turns on the phone again, punching in the number, known to him alone, of the cell phone entrusted to The Flounder. It rings for a good while before the other answers. "Yeah, hello?" says The Flounder. "Who's this? Oh, right, evening, Mr. B." On first impression, The Flounder's voice is not daisy fresh; it's a slow, torpid pulp, flat and vaguely somnolent, in which vowels heavily drag consonants behind them.

And at The Flounder's, where the light is as always very dim, the silhouette of the large fellow in dark clothes that Baumgartner met in the hallway is fiddling with God knows what on a pocket mirror using a Gillette razor blade, standing near the cassette player. We can't see a thing. The large, dark fellow smiles a hard smile while fiddling.

"What," says The Flounder, "what's wrong with my voice? No, of course I'm not on anything, I was just sleeping, that's all, I'm never alert when I just wake up. Are you?" (The large, dark fellow silently mimics disproportionate hilarity, nonetheless making sure not to expel any air for fear of scattering the two thin white rails before his eyes.) "The problem is that I'm going to need a bit more cash." (The dark fellow nods energetically.) "What do you mean, no way?" (The fellow knits his brow.) "But, oh, wait a minute! How do you like that, he hung up on me."

After hanging up, Baumgartner packs his suitcase. As he spends some time meticulously choosing his garments, each one as a function of the others, and as he takes advantage of the situation to examine his entire wardrobe, the operation takes him over an hour, but he has all the time in the world: he's not leaving Paris until early evening. He'll follow the belt road up to the Port d'Orléans exit, which will lead him to the highway, and so on toward southwestern France via Poitiers, where he'll spend the night.

Over the following weeks, Baumgartner will wander

like a vacationer throughout the Aquitaine region, alone, changing his hotel every third night, sleeping rigorously alone. He will not seem to obey any particular design, act according to any specific plan. Soon, venturing less and less out of the Pyrénées-Atlantiques area, he'll pass the time by exploring the few museums he finds, visiting churches every morning, running through all the tourist sites, and going in the afternoons to empty movie houses to see foreign films dubbed in French. Sometimes he'll drive aimlessly for hours, scarcely looking at the countryside, barely listening to the Spanish radio stations, and stopping only to take a leak on the shoulder, against a tree, or into a ditch. Sometimes he'll spend the entire day in his hotel room, facing stacks of magazines and TV shows.

Baumgartner, who apparently has gone away out of discretion, who seems eager to pass unnoticed, will be careful to speak with as few people as possible; but, if only so as not to lose the use of language, he will still call his wife every evening and The Flounder every four or five days. Apart from that, whether in Clos Zéphyr (Bayonne), Résidence des Meulières (near Anglet), or the Hotel Albizzia (outskirts of Saint-Jean-de-Luz), he never approaches anyone.

16

Either a terrified rabbit running full tilt at dawn over a vast, flat, grassy surface. Or a ferret named Winston who is chasing this rabbit. The latter, spotting the entrance to his lair not far off, naively imagines that he's out of the woods and that therein lies his salvation. But scarcely has he dived in, rushing all the way to the bottom to take refuge, than the ferret in hot pursuit catches him at this dead end, grabs him by the carotid, and bleeds him to death in the blackness. Then, taking his time, he drains him and stuffs himself on the other creature's blood, as attested by slight crackings from fractures and obscene sucking noises. Sated, looking forward to a well-deserved nap, the ferret then falls asleep beside his prey.

Or else two technicians of the Paris Airports who are waiting near the entrance to the lair. When they decide that the nap has lasted long enough, they call the ferret several times by name. Winston reappears after a moment, eye heavy with reproach and dragging the body of the rabbit, in whose neck he has planted his incisors like staples. The technicians grab the corpse by the ears before shutting Winston the ferret back in his cage. Debating as always the questions of how to divvy up the rabbit, how to cook it, what sauce to make, they climb into a small electric vehicle and ride off between the airport runways, on one of which Flight QN560 arriving from Montreal has just landed, and from which Ferrer disembarks, aching mightily and stiff with jet lag.

He'd had to stay longer than expected in Port Radium. Warmly adopted by the Aputiarjuk family, at whose home he had ended up taking all his meals and whose daughter, every night, came to join him in his bed, he had somewhat neglected the manufacture of his containers. For a few days, even, truth be told, such was the sweetness of the Aputiarjuk household that he had not really thought much at all about his antiques. Happy days in Port Radium. But once the containers were finished, he'd had to get ready to leave. Ferrer was a bit afraid to be disappointing, as usual, but the Aputiarjuk parents hadn't put up a fuss when they understood he wasn't going to be their son-in-law, and the farewells, all things considered, were fairly jolly.

Loading a Twin Otter, of the small two-engine model used in polar regions; dealing with customs in Montreal—all that had taken some time. Then the day of his return to France had come and here he was. It was another Sunday, in the first weeks of July, early in the morning. The nocturnal labors of sweeping, cleansing, scrubbing, and polishing the airport had just ended; the escalators and conveyor belts started back up in a long concert of murmurs.

At that hour, almost no one was working except for the customs agents and airport doctors, too busy with a party of pseudo-jewelers from Pakistan and so-called tourists from Colombia to get especially inter-

ested in Ferrer. X-raying these nationals, then gorging
them with laxatives to make them expel their precious
stones and pessaries of cocaine, and then, with sour
faces, slipping on gloves to recover these objects, they
also had occasion to track smugglers of trapdoor spi-
ders and boa constrictors, cartons of blond tobacco
buried in manioc flour, fissionable products, and con-
traband. Given the crowd that morning, Ferrer didn't
have too much trouble crossing the freight zone bottle-
necked with suspect packages; he passed through ignored by barrages of policemen and Finance Ministry
employees. Then, once his containers had been recovered, he had to call for a van to come load them. The
fact that it was Sunday made it a bit complicated,
but Rajputek, startled awake, finally agreed to come,
though not without some grumbling. While waiting for
his ride, Ferrer went back again to bide his time in the
foyer of the Spiritual Center.

Symmetrical to the Business Center with respect to
the Multistore, the Spiritual Center was located in the
airport basement, between the elevator and the esca-
lator. The foyer was rather cold and furnished with
metal armchairs, display racks stuffed with brochures
in seven languages, and troughs in which five varieties
of plants grew. The flaps of three half-open doors were
marked with a cross, a star, or a crescent, depending.
Sitting in an armchair, Ferrer took stock of the other
accessories: a wall phone, a fire extinguisher, a collection box.

As few people were there that early morning, Ferrer
hazarded three glances through the half-openings. The

microsynagogue was all but bare, three chairs around a low table. Same thing in the microchapel, with the addition of a flowerpot, altar, portrait of the Virgin, guest book accompanied by a ballpoint pen and two handwritten notices: one mentioned the presence of the Blessed Sacrament, the other bade visitors not to steal the Bic. As for the micromosque, it revealed a green carpet, a coat stand, and a mat next to which waited some Adidas, sandals, moccasins, and rubber overshoes from North African, Central African, and Middle Eastern believers.

As the morning progressed, the clientele of the Spiritual Center appeared little by little. It was composed less of passengers in transit than of airport employees, maintenance and upkeep staff in blue overalls, and security men, often black and always well built, walkie-talkies and beepers around their necks. Still, some civilian users also passed through: a pretty Lebanese nun; a Bulgarian mother with her large son; a small young man, frail and bearded, with Ethiopian physiognomy, his red eyes expressing a horror of the void, a fear of airsickness. Before boarding he wished to receive the sacrament from a priest that, regretfully, Ferrer confessed he wasn't.

Rajputek's van showed up toward the end of the morning. Once the containers were loaded, then unloaded at the gallery and carefully stocked in the studio, Ferrer returned to his domicile on foot. Leaving the gallery to head home, he cast a glance at the evolution of the construction site: it seemed that the foundations had been dug, they had installed metal huts to shelter the machines and men, they were beginning to mount two huge yellow cranes with the help of a superlative red crane. The noise level that week threatened to be infernal; we'll see.

In the meantime, on this summer Sunday, the silence of Paris was reminiscent of that on the ice floe, except that now it wasn't ice but tar that the sun superficially melted. As he approached his door, once at his floor, the absence of Extatics Elixir surprised him, as if the urban silence had made everything disappear, even decimating the tribe of perfumes. When he asked the concierge, he learned that in his absence Bérangère Eisenmann had moved out. So no more immediately available woman. Ferrer took it moderately well and, undoing his bags, he came across the fur recovered from the *Nechilik*. It was completely rotted. The hairs were falling off in batches from the skin which, in normal temperature, had mutated into old glue, purulent and stiff. Ferrer went to throw it out before attacking the mail.

It was at first glance a mountain of mail but, once the bills were paid and the announcements, invitations, circulars, and magazines tossed, all that remained was a summons to court, three months away, on October 10, for a hearing with Suzanne in the context of their divorce proceedings. At that point, he would have no women left at all, but knowing him, this state won't last. It shouldn't be long now.

17

What do you know: not two days have passed and here's one already. On Tuesday morning, Ferrer had an appointment with the appraiser, who arrived flanked by a man and a woman—his assistants. The expert appraiser was named Jean-Philippe Raymond, fifty-something, swarthy, sharp outline of a hunting knife draped in oversized clothes, confused elocution, dubious pout, and pointed stare. He moved with an unstable, unbalanced caution, steadying himself on the backs of chairs as on a bulwark during a Force 9 on the Beaufort scale. Having called upon the expert's services two or three times in the past, Ferrer already knew him a bit. The male assistant walked with more assurance, to which he added the continuous extraction of roasted peanuts from deep within his pocket and the wiping of his fingers on a translucent Kleenex every five minutes. As for the female assistant, who must have been going on thirty, she answered coldly to the name of Sonia. Blonde with beige eyes and a handsome, austere face denoting ice or embers, black suit and cream blouse, her hands busied themselves nonstop with a pack of Bensons on one side, an Ericsson mobile phone on the other.

Ferrer motioned them toward their chairs before unpacking the objects come in from the cold. Having

managed to sit, Jean-Philippe Raymond began to examine these antiques poutingly, without emitting any
comments, only delivering now and again esoteric coded
indications, series of figures and letters. Standing behind him, Sonia whispered these indications into the
Ericsson toward who knows what destination, then
whispered in return the equally abstract replies provided by her interlocutor, then lit another Benson.
After which, the expert and his other assistant delib-
erated obscurely while Ferrer, having given up trying to
understand anything at all, exchanged more than one
look with Sonia.

We all know these exchanges, these intrigued glances
addressed at first sight but with insistence by two
strangers who immediately please each other in a
group. These glances are instantaneous but serious and
vaguely disquieted, brief though prolonged; their du-
ration seems much greater than it really is. They slip
quietly into group conversations, while the group in
question doesn't notice anything, or pretends not to.
They provoke some upset in any case, since the assistant Sonia appeared once to confuse the functions of
her accessories, talking for two seconds into her Bensons.

The appraisal took nearly an hour, without either
man turning even once toward Ferrer, but at its end
Jean-Philippe Raymond's mouth twisted into a worri-
some grimace. The corners of his lips inflected toward
the floor as he added up several columns of signs in a
thin notebook bound in purple lizard, peevishly shak-
ing his head all the while, and Ferrer, seeing the man's

expression, thought it was a total loss: the entire lot isn't worth shit; all that traveling for nothing. But then the expert delivered his estimation. This sum, although stated after taxes and in a sour tone, easily rivaled the sale price of one or two small castles in the Loire Valley. Now, I'm not saying the great chateaux, like your Chambord or Chenonceaux; I'm talking about the small-to-medium-sized ones in the Montcontour or Talcy vein, which are already not bad.

"You have a safe, of course," the expert assumed.

"Goodness, no," answered Ferrer. "A safe. No. Or actually, yes, yes I do, an old one in back, but it's a bit small."

"You will have to lock all this up in a safe," Jean-Philippe Raymond pronounced gravely. "In a large safe. You can't keep it here. And it wouldn't be a bad idea to meet with your insurance agent as soon as possible. You don't have a safe, but you do have insurance, don't you?"

"Well," said Ferrer, "I'll look into all of that tomorrow."

"If I were you," Raymond said, standing up, "I wouldn't wait until tomorrow, but as you wish. I'm off now. Sonia will stay here to go over the appraisal fees. You can handle everything with her."

Handle everything with her, thought Ferrer. Of course.

"And how's business, otherwise?" asked Raymond in an indifferent voice while pulling on his coat. "The gallery?"

"It's going well," Ferrer assured him. "I have a few

stars," he ventured, hoping to impress Sonia. "But stars I can't exhibit every two years, right? They're too much in demand. I also have a few up-and-comers, but that's another problem, you know? With up-and-comers you can't start showing them too often too soon, people get tired of them too fast, so I show a piece or two of theirs now and then, no more. What would be good," he went on, "would be to mount a little exhibit for them sometimes, on the upper floor, that is if I had an upper floor, anyway you see what I mean, but it's going fine, it's going just fine." He interrupted himself there, aware that he was talking into the void and that everyone had begun to look elsewhere.

Still, once the matter of appraisal fees was handled, it would not be too difficult to invite Sonia to dinner— Sonia who, while letting nothing show, was actually pretty impressed. It was warm out; it would be good to dine outside, where the story of Ferrer's journey would hardly fail to interest the young woman to the highest degree—so high a degree, that she would turn off her Ericsson and light more and more Bensons—then he would accompany her back to her place, a little duplex not far from Quai Branly. And after they had agreed to have one last drink, when Ferrer followed her inside, the lower floor of her duplex turned out to be occupied by a young woman with dead eyes behind large bifocals, immersed in mimeographs of constitutional law supporting three empty containers of citrus-flavored yogurt, as well as a small receiving device in bright pink plastic that looked like a toy. A harmonious and nonviolent atmosphere reigned in that apartment. Red and pink cushions floated on a sofa upholstered in glazed flowered percale. On a tray, under soft lamplight, oranges cast shadows fuzzy as peaches.

The young woman and Sonia exchanged news of Bruno, whom Ferrer gathered was sleeping, age one and three-quarters, on the upper floor: the function of the bright pink monitor called Babyphone was to receive and transmit his possible cries. The baby-sitter took a ridiculous amount of time gathering up her documents, throwing her yogurt containers in the trash, and unplugging the Babyphone before finally leaving, and they could fall into each other and move around as if doing a clumsy lopsided dance like two enlaced crabs toward Sonia's room, where her unhooked black bra landed gently on the rug like a giant pair of sunglasses.

After a moment, reinstalled tautly on the bedside table, the Babyphone started to emit a shrill series of sighs and moans, at first light and in counterpart to Sonia's more or less soprano ones, but soon covering them over in a crescendo of wails, cries, and strident screeches. Immediately they disentangled themselves, not entirely willingly, before Sonia clambered upstairs to pacify young Bruno.

Left on his own and tempted to fall asleep, Ferrer deemed it practical and discreet before anything else to turn down the sound on the Babyphone. But not being familiar with this type of device, he no doubt pushed the wrong button, for instead of lowering the volume of cries and consolations, he changed the frequency, which abruptly intersected with that of the local guardians of the peace, whose nocturnal efforts of prevention, surveillance, and repression he could then follow perfectly clearly. No chance now of disabling the mechanism. Ferrer started frantically pressing every button he could find, looking for an antenna to twist off or a wire to cut, attempting to muffle the thing under a pillow, but in vain: on the contrary, each maneuver only amplified its vociferations, which were swelling by the second. Ferrer finally threw up his hands, threw on his clothes, and ran out, doing up his last buttons in the stairwell, not even needing to flee quietly, so completely did the clamors from the Babyphone invade the area, progressively spreading throughout the building—he would not be calling Sonia the next day.

On the other hand, Martine Delahaye, his former assistant's widow, whom Ferrer had met at the funeral, did call him the very next day. It had seemed to him that despite her mourning she had not found him entirely uninteresting, but at the time he figured it was only as a potential shoulder to cry on. Now, here she was phoning in late afternoon, on some indifferent pretext, some story about social security papers that Delahaye might have left at the gallery, can't find them for the life of her, and did he perhaps . . .

"Alas, I'm pretty sure he didn't," said Ferrer. "He never left his personal effects here."

"Oh, that's very distressing," said Martine Delahaye. Could she come by and see him anyway, something about having a drink together, it would make her happy to share some memories.

"It's a bit difficult right now," lied Ferrer, who especially did not want to envision any kind of scene with the widow Delahaye. "I've just gotten back from a trip and I have to leave again very soon, you see, I don't really expect to have much time."

"Too bad, that's a shame," said Martine Delahaye. "Did you go far?"

And Ferrer, to atone in his own mind for his fib, gave her a cursory recap of his trip to the Great North.

"Magnificent," enthused the widow, "I've always dreamed of seeing those places."

"It sure is beautiful," Ferrer said inanely. "No doubt about it, it sure is beautiful."

"How lucky you are," the widow exclaimed, "to be able to take your vacation in such a place."

"You know," replied Ferrer, a bit ruffled, "it wasn't really a vacation. Business trip, you know? I was after some things for the gallery."

"Magnificent!" she reiterated with ardor. "And did you find any?"

"I think I came back with a few small items," Ferrer said cautiously, "but we'll have to see. I don't have any exact appraisals yet."

"I would love to see them," said Martine Delahaye. "When will they be on view?"

"I couldn't really say for now," said Ferrer. "I haven't set any dates, but I can send you an invitation."

"Please do," said the widow. "Send me an invitation. You promise?"

"Sure," said Ferrer. "I promise."

For the entire period in question, Baumgartner had thus lived only in comfortable inns, residences, and other hosteleries copiously starred in the guidebooks. In July, for example, he had spent forty-eight hours at the Hotel Albizzia, where he had arrived toward the end of the afternoon. Four hundred twenty francs a night with continental breakfast. The room wasn't too bad at first glance: a bit large but nicely proportioned, and a velvety light slid in through a 16×9 bay window laced with climbing roses. Anatolia carpet, multi-functional shower head, erotic videos for rent, fawn-colored coverlet, and a view of a small park populated with starlings, wooded with hostage eucalyptus and imported mimosas.

If the mind-numbing starlings, having built their nests under the shingles of the Albizzia, in a hole in the wall, or in a eucalyptus, expressed themselves, as always, in whistles, creaks, clicks, and parodies of their feathered colleagues, they also seemed to have enriched their song: adapting to the present-day sonorous environment, not content with integrating into their repertoire the sounds of electronic games, musical car horns, and jingles from private radios, they had now added the cry of the portable telephone by which Baumgartner, as he did every three days, called The Flounder before going to bed early with a book.

Then it was with a newspaper that he went downstairs, fairly early the next morning, to have breakfast in the empty restaurant. No one was there at that hour. The sounds of clinking utensils and muffled voices reached him from the kitchen, rustlings, and dull footsteps of no interest: he pushed his glasses back up his nose without raising his head from the paper.

But now, for example, a few weeks later, Baumgartner has checked into another hotel farther north, the Résidence des Meulières, near Anglet. Here there is no garden but rather a paved courtyard lined with ancient sycamores, between which gurgles a small fountain, or rather a large water spout that lollops from side to side while producing an irregular frothy noise. Most of the time, it seems that this noise is trying to mimic moderate salvos of applause, sparse, unenthusiastic, or purely out of politeness. But occasionally it enters into synchrony with itself and for a few instants produces that binary, somewhat ridiculous rhythm of regular handclapping—more, more—that breaks out when the public demands the artist's return onstage.

As every day, Baumgartner calls his wife, but this time the telephone interview lasts longer than usual. Baumgartner asks a fair number of questions, jots down the answers in the margins of his newspaper, then ends the call. Reflects. Reestablishes the dial tone and dials The Flounder's number. The Flounder answers immediately.

"All right," Baumgartner tells him, "I think we can

get started. The first thing you do is rent a small refrigerated van. Not a truck, mind you, just a van."

"No problem," says The Flounder. "Why refrigerated?"

"Never mind about that," says Baumgartner. "Let's
just say it's to avoid breaking the cold chain. Here's a
number in Paris for you to take down. I'm coming
back tomorrow for a few days. Call me as soon as it's
done."

"Gotcha," says The Flounder, "understood. I'll take
care of it tomorrow and call you right away."

19

Isn't it about time Ferrer settled down? Will he forever accumulate these sorry affairs, whose outcome he knows in advance, about which he no longer even imagines, as he once did, that this time it's for real? Now he seems to give up at the first obstacle: after that business with Extatics Elixir, he didn't even think of looking up Bérangère's new address, and after the Babyphone episode he never tried to see Sonia again. Can he really have grown so blasé?

Meanwhile, since he had some time to spare, he went back to see the cardiologist about his latest results. "We're going to do that little ECG I told you about," Feldman said. "Come with me." The room was plunged in a light shadow pierced by three computer screens, though you could still see three awful reproductions on the walls, two angiology diplomas awarded to Feldman by foreign institutions, and a frame containing, under glass, photographs of his loved ones, including a dog. Ferrer undressed and lay down, naked except for his undershorts, on the examination bed covered with absorbent blue paper. He shivered a little despite the heat. "Relax your muscles, lie back," Feldman said after programming his machines.

Then the cardiologist began applying the tip of a black oblong, a sort of electronic pencil coated in conductive gel, to various parts of Ferrer's body, different places on his neck, underarms, thighs, ankles, and the corners of his eyes. Each time the pencil touched one of these areas, the noise of amplified arterial pounding sounded loudly in the computer's baffles, frightening sounds that were at once part sonar murmur, part brief gust of violent wind, the barking of a stuttering bulldog, or the panting of a Martian. So Ferrer listened to his arteries while, synchronically, wave flashes delivering their image appeared as peaks parading across the screen.

The whole thing lasted for a good while, then: "Not so great," Feldman observed, pulling Ferrer from the bed where he was reclining and tossing him another sheet of absorbent blue paper that he wiped over his body to mop up the smears of sticky gel. "Really not so great," Feldman repeated. "Goes without saying you'll have to be careful from now on. You're going to pay a little more attention to that diet I put you on. And forgive me for being blunt, but you're going to have to stop fucking around so much for a while."

"Well, that shouldn't be a problem," said Ferrer.

"One more thing," said Feldman. "Avoid exposure to extreme temperatures, not too cold or too hot. It can be disastrous for someone in your condition. Anyway," he snickered, "I don't suppose you get much opportunity for that in your line of work."

"Right you are," said Ferrer, not uttering a word about his trip to the extreme North.

Right now it's a July morning. The city is relatively quiet; a climate of unexpressed mourning reigns over everything, and Ferrer is sitting alone at a sidewalk café in Place Saint-Sulpice with a beer. All things considered, it's a good distance from Port Radium to Saint-Sulpice, a healthy half-dozen hours of jet lag from which Ferrer still hasn't recovered. Despite Jean-Philippe Raymond's admonitions, he has put off finding a safe and insurance; he'll make those appointments later, at the end of the afternoon. In the meantime, he's stored all the antiques in a locked closet, at the far end of the back room that also has a lock. For the moment he's resting, though no one ever really rests. People sometimes say, they imagine that they are resting or are going to rest, but it's really just a vain hope. They know perfectly well that it won't work, that true rest doesn't even really exist; it's just something to say when you're tired.

Although run down, a bit weary of it all, Ferrer does not forgo watching women pass by, so scantily clad in this season, so immediately desirable that sometimes it almost hurts, like a ghost of pain in the solar plexus. One is, at times, so tempted by the spectacle of the world that one could even forget about one's best interests. The very beautiful and the not-so-beautiful alike: Ferrer watches them all. He savors the absent, slightly haughty, dominating look the very beautiful ones assume. But he also likes the absent, slightly haggard, wincing, downward-plunging gaze the not-so-pretty ones adopt when they know perfectly well that someone is scrutinizing them from the sidewalk of a bar because he's found nothing better to do and that, moreover, he's judging them not so bad to look at as they think. All the more so in that they, too, must make love, like everyone else, and no doubt their faces become quite different, that's a fact; and perhaps then the hierarchy of very beautiful and not-so-pretty is no longer the same at all. But Ferrer's thoughts must not take such a turn: Feldman has forbidden it.

At that same moment, The Flounder is walking toward a huge private parking lot, guarded by massive watchmen flanked by huge dogs, out past the peripheral boulevard behind Porte de Champerret. While walking, The Flounder breathes more easily than before. When his skin itches, he scratches himself distractedly, but it's not an unpleasant sensation. And so he can walk for a long time in the sun; he moves forward. He passes by a small, basic garage—workbenches, a drainage trough, three cars inelegantly deboned, a winch: nothing special. Then comes the parking lot, which apparently specializes in utilitarian vehicles: eighteen-wheelers, trailers, semi-trailers. In his transparent cage, where he reigns over six video-surveillance screens and two full ashtrays, the parking lot attendant is small, compact as a battery, and friendly as a toothache. The Flounder announces that he's come for the refrigerated van someone should have reserved by phone the day before. The man nods, apparently in the know; he leads The Flounder to the object in question.

It's a white parallelepiped delivery van, all square corners like a box or the huts of Port Radium: its body is not designed to fly through the air. Over the cab a small motor is installed, capped with a circular ventilation grill that looks like a hot plate. The attendant unlocks the back doors, revealing a vast, empty space with metal walls; several Styrofoam coolers are stacked in the rear. Although the inside is clean and probably scrubbed down with disinfectant, it still gives off a slight odor of stale grease, insipid blood, aponeurosis, and ganglion. No doubt it is normally used to transport wholesale meats.

After half-listening to the attendant explain how the vehicle works, The Flounder hands him part of the money entrusted by Baumgartner and lets him slide open the cab door before climbing aboard. Once the man leaves, The Flounder pulls from his pocket a pair of extra-thick yellow rubber household gloves, whose textured palms and thumbs grip surfaces, preventing objects from slipping. The Flounder puts them on, then turns the ignition key and starts up. Reverse sticks a bit, but after that the gears shift harmoniously as the truck heads toward the outer peripheral boulevard, which we'll leave at Porte de Châtillon.

At Place de la Porte de Châtillon, The Flounder double-parks the van in front of a telephone booth. He climbs down from the vehicle, enters the booth, picks up the phone, and utters a few words. He appears to receive a brief reply, then, leaving behind several molecules of himself—fragment of earwax blocking a hole in the receiver, drop of saliva in an orifice of the speaker—he hangs up with one eyebrow raised. He does not look very convinced. He even seems a trifle wary.

20

Baumgartner, on the other end, hangs up without registering any particular expression. *He* doesn't look displeased as he heads toward a studio window: not much to see; he opens the window: not much to hear—the songs of two birds chasing after each other, a faraway haze of automobile traffic. So he has returned to Paris, come back to his large studio on Boulevard Exelmans with no facing windows. He has nothing left to do but wait, kill time by staring out the window, and when night falls he'll stare at the television. But for now it's the window.

The paved courtyard, planted with lindens and acacias, contains a small garden edged with shrubs that encircle a basin with a vertical spout of water, arched over today, not to say driven a little crazy, by a slight breeze. Several sparrows, two or three blue jays or blackbirds animate the trees. A blob of whitish plastic emblazoned with the name of a hardware store, caught in a tangle of tall branches and inflated by that breeze like a small sail, vibrates and trembles like an organism while emitting clacks and kazoo sounds. Below him, overturned, lies a child's bike with training wheels. Three inconsequential streetlamps set in the corners of the courtyard and three video-surveillance cameras installed above the doors of the villas keep watch over this little panorama.

Although the branches of the linden tree block visibility from one villa to the next, Baumgartner can make out the decks with their striped lawn chairs and teak tables, the balconies and large bay windows, the sophisticated TV antennas. Farther beyond, he glimpses a row of opulent buildings presenting various architectural disparities, but no matter, nothing clashes: 1910 blends smoothly with 1970 in harmonious coexistence, money winning out over anachronism every time.

The occupants of these villas apparently share the common ground of being roughly forty-five years old and of making a good living in various audiovisual domains. There is, in a blue office, a fat young woman wearing fat headphones, typing into her computer the text of a local-interest program that Baumgartner has already listened to, mornings at around eleven, on one of the public radio stations. There's a short redheaded fellow with an absent look and fixed smile, who does not extricate himself very often from the deck chair on his terrace and who must be a producer or something, since when it comes to girls the man's got a nonstop parade. There's a television war correspondent who isn't home much, spending her life on the sites of every conflict, hopping from one landmine to the next with her satellite telephone, from the Khmer to the Chechens and from the Yemenites to the Afghans. Since she's mainly asleep when she's home, Baumgartner doesn't see her too often, except sometimes on his screen.

For the moment he doesn't see anyone. Earlier that

morning, behind the Vietnamese embassy, five or six diplomats in jogging suits were doing their tai chi, as they do every day. But right now, on the other side of the embassy fence, there's nothing but a basketball backboard nailed to a tree, an asymmetrical swing, and a rusted safe turned over on its back, against an empty cement wall with an empty chair set in front. It seems to be warmer, more humid on that side of the fence, as if the embassy produced its own Southeast Asian microclimate.

Baumgartner, in any case, looks at the world only from a distance. Though he watches people, in public he plays dead and doesn't greet anyone, except, every Monday, while handing him his voluminous rent, the retired dentist on the ground floor who leases him his upper floor by the week. They have made this arrangement, Baumgartner having notified the dentist from the start that he would not be staying long, that he would probably have to leave on a minute's notice. Still, it's a fact that, cloistered in his studio most of the time and getting rather bored, he has to go out for some air now and again.

Here he is, in fact, taking a walk and, well well, here's the war correspondent, seemingly awake, heading off with a yawn to some editorial meeting. She's one of those tall blondes who drive an Austin Mini; hers is emerald green with a white roof, dented grill, windows spangled with towing notices that the police chief, a friend, will fix for her. It's just that this is a wealthy neighborhood inhabited by a fair number of well-known people, who themselves know a fair number of well-known people; a nice neighborhood, also frequented by a fair number of tabloid photographers.

And indeed, two of them are lurking under a porch-way on Rue Michel-Ange, armed with fat oblong devices made of gray plastic that look less like cameras than like telescopes, periscopes, musical instruments, or even weapons with infrared sights. The paparazzi are startlingly young and dressed as if for the beach, in short-sleeved shirts and Bermuda shorts, but their faces are solemn as they watch the porch across the street; no doubt they're waiting for a superstar to come out with her new flame. Baumgartner stops out of curiosity; he waits a moment with them, discreetly and without showing any interest, until one of the photographers suggests none too politely that he shove off. He's not contrary; he leaves.

He is idle, almost painfully idle. He'll go take a spin around the Auteuil cemetery, which is nearby and of modest proportions, housing the remains of a fair number of Englishmen, barons, and sea captains. A few tombstones are broken, left abandoned, while others are being restored; one of the funerary monuments that looks like a small villa, decorated with statues and the verb *Credo* in place of a doormat, seems to be undergoing renovation. Baumgartner walks without stopping past Delahaye's tomb—though he retraces his steps to right an overturned pot of azaleas—past the grave of a stranger who was doubtless hard of hearing—*Homage from his deaf friends in Orléans*, shouts the slab—then past the grave of Hubert Robert—*Dutiful son, tender spouse, good father, loyal friend,* murmurs the slab—and that's quite enough: he leaves the Auteuil cemetery and walks back up Rue Claude-Lorrain toward Michel-Ange.

There, a little later, as the long-awaited superstar has just crossed the porch with her new flame, the two photographers start bombarding the couple. The flame wiggles and smiles beatifically, the superstar freezes and directs the photographers to Hell, and Baumgartner, returning from the cemetery and wrapped up in his own thoughts, walks absentmindedly through their field of vision on his way back home. Once there, he pours himself a drink and stares out the window again, waiting for the end of day that takes its time, that infinitely stretches the shadows of things stationary and vegetal, porch steps and acacias, until both they and their shadows are engulfed by a larger shadow that softens their contours and colors, to the point of absorbing them, imbibing them, extinguishing them, making them disappear, and that's when the phone rings.

"It's me," says The Flounder. "It went off like a charm."

"You're sure no one saw you?" worries Baumgartner.

"Get out," scoffs The Flounder. "There was nobody in back. To tell the truth, there was hardly anybody in the front room, either. You ask me, this modern art stuff doesn't seem to be doing so hot."

"Shut up, you moron," says Baumgartner. "What else? Where's the stuff now?"

"Everything's in the fridge, just like we planned,"

answers The Flounder. "It's parked all snug and warm near my place, in the storage space you rented. So what do we do now?"

"We meet tomorrow at Charenton," says Baumgartner. "You remember the address?"

All this time Ferrer is still nursing a beer, the same and then another under the sun, but if he hasn't changed neighborhoods on the left bank, he has nonetheless changed cafés. He is now sitting in Carrefour de l'Odéon, which is not usually the ideal spot for having a drink even though you can always find people there whose lives are devoted to it: it's an agitated, enclosed, noisy hub, stuffed with red lights and cars heading in all directions at once, and moreover it's chilled by the great drafts of air that come from Rue Danton. But in summer, when Paris has cleared out a little, the side-walk cafés are relatively bearable, the light is steady and the traffic calmer, and there is an unobstructed view of two entrances to the same metro station. A parade of people comes and goes from these entrances and Ferrer watches it pass by, taking a closer interest in the female half of this parade, which is, at least quan-titatively, as we know, superior to the other half.

This female half could also, he's noticed, be subdi-vided into two populations: those who, just after you leave them (not necessarily forever), look back as you watch them walk down the subway stairs, and those who (forever or not) do not look back. As for Ferrer, he always looks back the first time to judge in which camp, looker or non-looker, a new acquaintance belongs. Then he takes his cue from her, conforms to her mannerisms, models his behavior on hers, given that it really doesn't do any good to look back if the other doesn't.

But today no one is looking back and Ferrer is about to head home. As no available taxi presents itself—roof lights dark, off-duty signs on—and as time generously permits, it is perfectly reasonable to return home on foot. It's a bit far but it can be done, and a little exercise can only help put some order in Ferrer's thoughts, still muddled by the last remnants of his jet lag.

These thoughts, in no particular order, and not counting memories, concern the insurance agent and safe dealer he has to call, a stand-maker's bill to be renegotiated, Martinov whom he really should repromote, given that for now he's his only relatively prominent artist. Then there's the lighting in the gallery, which has to be totally redesigned to go with the new antiques. And finally he forces himself to ponder whether or not he's going to call Sonia.

And the urban spectacle, in order, as he approaches Rue d'Amsterdam, zigzagging along the sidewalks amid the dog turds, notably presents a guy in dark glasses pulling a large drum out of a white Rover, a little girl declaring to her mother that, all things considered, she's opted for the trapeze, then two women about to slit each other's throats over a parking spot, followed by a refrigerated truck speeding away.

Arriving at the gallery, Ferrer is detained a moment by an artist who comes at Rajputek's recommendation and who wants to tell Ferrer about his projects. He's a young plastic artist, smug and self-satisfied, who has zillions of friends in the art world, and his projects are of the kind Ferrer has also seen by the zillions. The trick this time is that, instead of hanging a painting on a wall, he eats away at the corresponding place in the collector's wall with acid: small rectangular format, nine by twelve inches and one and a quarter inches deep. "I'm exploring the concept of the negative work, so to speak," the artist expounds. "I subtract from the wall's thickness instead of adding to it."

"Of course," says Ferrer. "It's interesting, but I'm not doing too much in that area at the moment. We might want to think about an arrangement, but later, not right now. We'll have to talk again. Leave me your book and I'll be in touch."

Once rid of the wall eater, Ferrer tries to settle all the pending matters, assisted by a young woman named Elisabeth whom he's hired on a trial basis to replace Delahaye and who is anorexic but overdosed with vitamins; she is there only on spec, we'll see how she works out. For starters, he gives her a few minor assignments.

Then it's back to the telephone: Ferrer calls the insurance man and the safe salesman, both of whom promise to come tomorrow. He reconsiders the bill from the stand-maker, whom he also calls, announcing his visit for later in the week. He doesn't manage to reach Martinov directly, gets only his answering machine on which he deposits an ingenious hodgepodge of admonishments, blandishments, and warnings—in short, he does his job. He lengthily discusses with Elisabeth the best way to improve the lighting in the gallery, in view of exhibiting the Polar objects. To clarify his ideas, Ferrer suggests going to fetch one or two in the studio, we'll try it out with, let's say, the ivory armor and one of the mammoth tusks, you'll see what I mean, Elisabeth. Then he heads toward the back of the gallery, unlocks the door to the studio, and that's all there is to it: forced, gaping, the closet door opens onto nothing. It's no longer the moment to think about whether he's going to call Sonia.

22

Leaving two fat buckled valises just inside the entrance to his perfectly tidy studio, as if he were preparing to vacate the premises in short order, Baumgartner slammed the door on his way out. Like a pitch pipe, a dial tone, or the signal announcing the automatic closing of subway doors, this curt, dull thud produced an almost perfect *A* that made the strings of the Bechstein baby grand ring in sympathy: for twenty seconds after Baumgartner left the place, the ghost of a major chord haunted the empty studio before slowly fading, then dissipating.

Baumgartner crossed Boulevard Exelmans, which he followed for a moment toward the Seine before cutting over onto Rue Chardon-Lagache. In the middle of summer, the 16th arrondissement is even more deserted than usual, to the point where Chardon-Lagache, at certain angles, affords postnuclear perspectives. Baumgartner retrieved his car from the underground lot of a modern building on Avenue de Versailles, then rejoined the Seine and took the express lane, which he left behind before the Sully bridge. He found himself at Place de la Bastille, from where he followed the long Rue de Charenton in a southeasterly direction, to the town of Charenton itself. He then crossed via its axis, along its spine, the entire 12th arrondissement, which is a little more populated in this season than the 16th, the population taking fewer vacations in the former than in the latter. On the sidewalks one can especially see, slow, solitary, and perplexed, third world natives and senior citizens.

Once in Charenton, the Fiat veered right into a small artery bearing the name Molière or Mozart, Baumgartner could never remember which, but he knew that it ended perpendicular to another fast-moving street, beyond which stretched a minuscule industrial zone bordering the Seine. This zone is composed of rows of warehouses, lines of garages with metal shutters, some of which carry the painted names of companies, stenciled or not. Indicated by a large sign—*Flexibility in the service of logistics*—there are also a number of storage cubicles for rent, ranging in surface area from twenty to ten thousand square feet. In addition, there are also two or three small, quiet factories that look as if they're operating at one-quarter capacity as well as a purification plant, all of this scattered around a stretch of apparently nameless road.

This sector is emptier still than anywhere else in the middle of summer, and almost silent: the only perceptible noises finish up as vague rumors, dull shudders, echoes of God knows what. During the year, at most, two elderly couples might walk their dogs there. Certain driving-school instructors have also spotted this place and spread the word, taking advantage of the zero traffic to let their charges maneuver at reduced risk, and sometimes also, vehicle on his shoulder, a cyclist crosses it to take the little bridge that spans the

Seine toward Ivry. From that footbridge one can see many other bridges cast in every direction above the waters. Just upstream from the confluence with the Marne, a large Chinese business and hotel complex raises its Manchurian architecture on the edge of the river and bankruptcy.

But today there is nothing and no one. Nothing but a refrigerated delivery van parked in front of one of the storage cubicles, no one but The Flounder at the wheel of that van equipped with a Thermo King. Baumgartner has parked the Fiat alongside the refrigerator and lowered his window without getting out of the car: it's The Flounder who has to extricate himself from the van. The Flounder is hot and The Flounder is complaining. Perspiration magnifies his sloppy appearance: his hair is a frizzy, greasy mess, sweat stains are superimposed onto the various spots on his message T-shirt, and grimy stripes bar his face like prefaces to wrinkles.

"All set," says The Flounder, "everything's here. What now?"

"Now you carry them," answers Baumgartner, handing him the key to the cubicle. "You stack everything in there. And be careful to handle these things gently."

"It's just that with this heat . . . ," The Flounder reminds him.

"Carry," Baumgartner repeats.

Behind his wheel, without leaving his seat and constantly assuring himself that no one is watching, Baumgartner slips on a pair of tanned gloves, supple and light to wear, sewn with linen thread, all the while supervising the transfer of the containers into the storage cubicle. It really is hot, not a breath of wind; The Flounder is swimming. His muscles decimated by toxins still roll a little under his T-shirt and Baumgartner does not like that, does not like looking at that, does not like the fact that he likes looking at that. Then, his labors finished, The Flounder walks back to the Fiat.

"All set," he says. "You want to see? Hey, you're wearing gloves."

"It's the weather," says Baumgartner, "it's me, it's this heat. It's dermatological. Don't worry about it. Are you sure you got everything?"

"Everything," says The Flounder.

"Wait while I make sure," says Baumgartner, who steps out of his car and inspects the contents of the cubicle. Then he raises his head, brows knit. "There's one missing," he says.

"One what?" says The Flounder.

"A container," says Baumgartner. "There's one that isn't there."

"You're joking," the addict exclaims. "There were seven to begin with and there are seven now. It's all set."

"I don't think so," says Baumgartner. "Go check inside the truck, you must have forgotten one."

The Flounder shrugs his shoulders doubtfully, then, as he climbs back into the refrigerator compartment, Baumgartner slams the van doors on him. Muffled voice of The Flounder, at first jocular, then distorted, then worried. Baumgartner locks the doors, walks around the refrigerated van, opens the driver's-side door, and sits behind the wheel.

From the cab, you no longer hear the young man's voice at all. Baumgartner opens a small shutter located behind the driver's seat, releases a catch, then slides open the rectangular peephole that allows communication with the isothermic compartment. This opening is half the size of a pack of cigarettes: while it allows you to look in back, it's too small to pass your hand through.

"There," says Baumgartner, "it's over now."

"Wait up," says The Flounder, "what are you doing? Stop screwing around, will you? Please?"

"It's over," Baumgartner repeats. "You are finally going to leave me in peace."

"I've never bothered you," The Flounder inanely observes. "Let me out now."

"I can't," says Baumgartner. "You do bother me. You are liable to bother me, therefore you bother me."

"Let me out," The Flounder says again, "or else people will find out and you'll be in trouble."

"I don't think so," says Baumgartner. "You have no legal existence, you understand. No one will notice anything. Even the cops won't care. Nobody knows you're alive except your pusher, who wouldn't be doing himself any favors by calling them. How do you expect anyone to notice you have no more existence at all? Who'll miss you? Come on, now, settle down. It'll all be over soon, just a little heat and cold."

"No!" says The Flounder. "No, and stop the monologue, if you don't mind." He tries again to convince

Baumgartner before running short of arguments. "And besides," he ventures as a last resort, "your whole deal is so cliché. They kill people like this in every TV movie in the world, there's nothing original about it at all."

"I don't disagree," Baumgartner allows, "but I admit to being influenced by TV movies. TV movies are an art form like any other. And anyway, that's enough now."

Then he hermetically seals the peephole and, after switching on the engine, activates the compressor. We all know the thermodynamic principle that governs an isothermic vehicle, and refrigerators in general: gas circulates in the walls, absorbing the heat contained inside. Thanks to a small motor located above the cab and the compressor that causes this gas to circulate, the heat is transformed into cold. Moreover, there exist two temperature options for vehicles of this type: $40°$ or $0°$. It's the latter type that Baumgartner, by telephone, has made sure to reserve two days earlier.

23

The disappearance of Ferrer's antiques obviously represented a heavy loss. Financing for the expedition to the Great North, in which he had invested a fair amount of capital, was gone, pure deficit. And as the time came when nothing was selling at the gallery—mediocre offerings combined with the slow season—it was of course also the moment his creditors chose to remind him of their existence, artists to demand their fees, and bankers to voice their concern. Then, when summer's end appeared on the horizon, as in each year at that time there would be no delay in the arrival of all kinds of taxes, threats of fiscal reform, various fees and dues, the renewal of his lease accompanied by registered letters from the building manager. Ferrer began to feel at bay.

Before anything else he had to file a complaint, of course. As soon as he'd noticed the theft, Ferrer had called the main police station of the 9th arrondissement and a weary officer from Criminal Investigations had shown up within the hour. The man had noted the damage, registered the complaint, and asked the name of his insurance company.

"Well, that is," Ferrer said, "it so happens that these objects weren't insured quite yet. I was about to see to it, but—"

"You're a prize imbecile," the policeman had crudely interrupted, making him feel ashamed of his negligence and pointing out that the fate of vanished objects was as uncertain as could be, the chances of finding them microscopic. This kind of case, he expounded, was rarely solved, given the highly organized nature of art smuggling: in the best of circumstances, the matter would drag on for a long time. They'd see what they could do, but they weren't off to a very good start. "Anyway, I'll send somebody from Criminal Records," the detective concluded, "see if he can come up with anything. Meanwhile, of course, you're to touch nothing."

The technician arrived a few hours later. He didn't introduce himself immediately, first spending a moment in the gallery to examine the art. He was a small, thin myope with overly fine blond hair, smiling continuously and not appearing all that eager to get to work. Ferrer had at first taken him for a potential client—"Are you interested in modern art?"—before the man identified himself, showing the insignia of his profession. Detective Paul Supin, Criminal Records Division.

"That must be fascinating," said Ferrer. "Your job."

"You know," the other said, "I'm just a lab technician. Take me away from my electron microscope and I don't really see much. But yes, it's true, I am interested in all this."

In Ferrer's studio he had unpacked his little kit, a tool box containing the classic accessories: camera, vials of transparent liquids, powder and tweezers, gloves. Ferrer watched him work until the other took his leave. He was demoralized, would have to start over quickly; it began to feel inordinately hot.

The summer progressed slowly, as if the heat had made time itself viscous, its passage seemingly impeded by the friction of its molecules raised to a high temperature. With most of the movers and shakers on vacation, Paris was more supple and sparse but no more breathable in the still air rich in toxic gases like a smoky bar before closing time. Here and there the city took advantage of the reduced traffic to dig up the streets and put them back together: rollings of jackhammers, rotations of steam drills, gyrations of cement mixers, flows of fresh tar in the sun veiled by various exhalations. To all this Ferrer paid scant attention: too many other things to think about as he crossed Paris in a taxi from one bank branch to another, trying without much success to borrow money, beginning to envision mortgaging the gallery. So it is that we find him at eleven in the morning, under the crushing heat, on Rue du 4-Septembre.

This Rue du 4-Septembre is very wide and very short and money is what makes it tick. All more or less the same, its Napoleon III–style buildings contain international and other kinds of banks, headquarters of insurance agencies, brokerage firms, temporary employment services, editorial offices of financial publications, currency exchange and appraisal offices, estate administrators, managing agents for co-ops, real estate storefronts, lawyers' offices, rare-stamp dealerships, and the charred debris of the Crédit Lyonnais. The only brasserie in the neighborhood is called L'Agio. But you can also find the head offices of a Polish airline, photocopying services, travel agencies and beauty institutes, a world-champion hairstylist, and a commemorative plaque to a Resistance man who gave his life for France at the age of nineteen (*In Memoriam*).

And there are also, on Rue du 4-Septembre, thousands of square feet of renovated office space for rent and uncompleted spaces under strict electronic surveillance: they gut the old buildings, preserving the facades, columns, and caryatids, the sculpted crowned heads overhanging the street entrances. They restructure the floors, adapting them to the laws of bureaucracy, and create spacious suites, scenic and double-paned, the better to accumulate more and still more capital. As everywhere in Paris in summer, hard-hatted workmen scurry around, unfold blueprints, bite into sandwiches, and express their views into walkie-talkies.

It was the sixth bank in two days that Ferrer had approached to solicit a loan; once again he walked out without success, his damp fingers leaving their imprints on the documents with which he had armed himself. After the aforesaid had let him down once again, the elevator doors opened at the ground floor onto a wide entrance foyer, containing no people but many sofas and low tables. As he walked across this space, Ferrer had neither the will nor the energy to go home right away; he preferred to sit for a moment on one of the sofas. What tells us, physically, that he was weary, pessimistic, or discouraged? The fact, for instance, that he kept his jacket on despite the heat; that he stared fixedly at a mote of dust on his sleeve without thinking to brush it off; that he did not even push back a lock of hair that had fallen into his eyes; but perhaps most of all, that he sat without reacting when a woman passed through the foyer.

Given this woman's appearance, this is the most surprising part. By all logic, as we slightly know him, Ferrer should have been interested. She was a tall, slender young woman with statuesque contours, well defined lips, long, light-green eyes, and wavy copper-colored hair. She was wearing high heels and a loose black ensemble, cut low in the back, decorated with small light-colored chevrons on her hips and shoulders.

As she passed near him, anyone else, or he himself in his normal frame of mind, would have judged that these clothes were there only to be taken off her, even ripped off her. The blue folder, moreover, that she was carrying under her arm, the pen that thoughtfully brushed against her lips seemed purely formal accessories, she herself looking like an actress in a hard-core porn film during the preliminary scenes, when people say anything at all while waiting for the situation to heat up. That said, she wore not a drop of makeup. Ferrer had just enough time to notice this detail, though without according it any more interest than to the decor of the foyer, when a pervasive weakness engulfed him, as if all the parts of his body were suddenly deprived of air.

A thousand-pound weight then seemed to crash down on his shoulders, skull, and chest all at once. A taste of sour metal and dry dust invaded his mouth, his forehead, filled his neck and throat, creating a stifling mixture: swelling of a sneeze, violent hiccup, profound nausea. It was impossible to react in any way whatsoever; his wrists seemed bound by handcuffs and his mind saturated by a feeling of suffocation, acute anxiety, and imminent death. Pain ripped through his chest, spiraling from his throat to his pelvis, from his navel to his shoulders, irradiating his left arm and leg, and he saw himself fall off the sofa, saw the floor rush up toward him at top speed, though at the same time in slow motion. Once he was lying on the ground, at first it was impossible to move; then, having lost his balance, he lost consciousness—for how long is impossible to know, but it was just after recalling for an instant what Feldman had warned him about regarding the effects of extreme temperatures on coronary cases.

He came to almost instantly, even though it was now impossible to utter a word: it was not blackness that engulfed the screen like a turned-off television, no, his field of vision continued to function the way a video camera fallen to the ground still goes on filming after the sudden death of its operator, and records in static shot whatever falls into its lens: a corner of wall and wooden flooring, a badly framed plinth, a piece of tiling, some excess glue at the edge of the rug. He wanted to stand but fell back more heavily still when he tried. Persons other than the young woman in black must have come running, for he felt them leaning over him, removing his jacket and laying him on his back, looking around for a telephone, then the firemen came quickly in their truck.

The firemen were handsome, strapping young fellows, calm and reassuring, equipped with navy blue uniforms, leather accessories, and snap hooks on their belts. Gently they settled Ferrer on a stretcher and precisely slid the stretcher into their truck. Ferrer felt protected now. Without thinking that this episode had more than a little in common with the one from February, albeit much less pleasant, he tried to recover the rudimentary use of speech in the fire truck, but he was kindly told to keep quiet until they reached the hospital. Which he did. Then he fainted again.

24

When Ferrer opened his eyes, at first he saw around him only white, like in the good old days of the ice floe. He was resting in an adjustable single bed with a firm mattress and tightly made up, alone in a small room, with no other color but the distant emerald of a tree standing out against the sky in the square frame of a window. The sheets, the bedcover, the walls of the room, and the sky itself were equally white. The faraway tree, the single green note, could have been one of the thirty-five thousand sycamores, the seven thousand lindens, or the thirteen thousand five hundred chestnut trees planted around Paris. Unless it was one of the ones you might come across in the last remaining deserted lots whose name no one ever remembered, which perhaps didn't even have a name, and which were no more than giant weeds, a clandestine flora monstrously gone to seed. Although it was too far away, Ferrer still tried to identify it, but this minor effort was enough to exhaust him and he shut his eyes again.

The next time he opened them, five minutes later or the next morning, the decor remained unchanged but this time Ferrer abstained from revisiting the question of the tree. It's hard to tell whether he forced himself to think of nothing or whether he was in no condition to ponder anything at all. As he felt and confusedly distinguished a small foreign body stuck to his nose that made him squint a bit, he tried bringing up his hand to identify it, but his right forearm did not respond. Further investigation revealed that this forearm was supine, attached to the head of the bed with a strap and pierced by a fat perfusion needle held in place by a wide translucent bandage. Ferrer began to understand what was going on; it was only for form's sake that he verified, with his left hand, that the external object attached under his nostrils was a breathing tube. It was then that the door opened and a young woman, also dressed in white but with black skin, stuck her head through the doorway, turned back toward what must have been a nurse's aide, and asked that person to notify Doctor Sarradon that number 43 was awake.

Alone once more, Ferrer timidly renewed his attempts to identify that tree in the distance, but, if he still couldn't manage, at least he didn't fall asleep this time: we were making progress. Nonetheless, it was cautiously that he inspected his surroundings in greater detail, turning his head to distinguish various machines at his bedside, screens and meters that must have been keeping track of his heart's condition: numbers in liquid crystal constantly trembling and changing, sine curves moving from left to right, always renewed, similar and different like ocean waves. A telephone sat on his nightstand and an oxygen mask hung from a hook. Ferrer made the best of the situation. Outside, daylight was waning, transforming all the white in his room into tannish gray and darkening the color of the far-away tree to bronze green, then forest green. Finally, the door opened again and this time it was Dr. Sarra-don himself, who wore a dense black beard and a bottle-green smock, with a paltry little skullcap of the same color: we're sticking with green.

While examining his patient, Sarradon explained that after his emergency admission to the hospital they'd had to perform a multiple bypass while he was still unconscious; everything seemed to have gone pretty smoothly. And in fact, once the sheets were turned down, as they were changing his bandages, Ferrer found that he was entirely resewn the length of his left arm and leg as well as from the meridian of the thorax. It was pretty like master craftsmanship, con-sisting in long, fine, regular sutures reminiscent of Re-naissance English lace or the back of a high-fashion stocking, or a line of writing.

"Good," pronounced the doctor at the end of his exam. "It's coming along fine," he added, scanning the charts that hung from the foot of the bed, while the nurse dressed Ferrer in highly bleached pajamas. At this point, according to Sarradon, the patient should spend another three or four days in the intensive care ward before moving to a normal room. Then he should be able to leave just two weeks after that. Visits al-lowed. Night was falling.

The next morning, in fact, Ferrer felt a little more himself. He spent a moment wondering who, among his acquaintances, he could tell of his situation. It was better not to notify Suzanne, who hadn't heard from him in over six months and who might not respond too well to his call. He also preferred not to risk alarming his family, who in any case seemed to have become a sparse and distant archipelago, gradually submerged by the rising waters. To tell the truth, that didn't leave too many people, and Ferrer promised himself to at least call the gallery that afternoon. Even though Elisabeth, quickly accustomed to his brief impromptu absences, must have opened the shop as usual and handled the day's business, it would be better if she knew where he was. But there was no rush. Besides, he was better off closing the gallery altogether during his convalescence, which wouldn't be such a bad idea in this off-season. He'd call her about it tomorrow. For now, he was going to try to get some sleep, when the nurse, contrary to expectation, announced that he had a visitor. Unthinkingly, Ferrer tried to sit up against the headboard, but no, still too weak, no can do.

A young woman then appeared, whom he had all the more difficulty recognizing in that she had changed since Rue du 4-Septembre: she was now wearing a blue tank top with rust-colored stripes and a high-slit skirt of a more sustained blue. And flat shoes. And one shoulder strap of the tank top had a tendency to slip off. Still, she was as unmade-up as before. When, after several seconds of confusion, he finally identified her, Ferrer did not feel presentable in his pajamas: he made an automatic gesture to comb his dirty hair that was weighed down, in slabs, by conductive solution from the routine electroencephalogram performed when he was admitted.

Despite the shoulder strap, regardless of the high slit, and even though this woman's bearing was very much of a sort to put ideas in your head, Ferrer felt from the start that nothing would ever happen between them. As much as he could look at the nurses, from the depths of his weakness and with half-closed eyes, and speculate on the presence or not of other textile elements under their blouses, so this woman inspired in him no more emotion than a Visitant—indeed, there was something almost religious about her lack of makeup. Unless he unconsciously felt that she was too good for the likes of him, such things do happen—but no, he's not really that type.

She wouldn't stay more than five or ten minutes, in any case, explaining that she had gotten the name of the hospital from the firemen, that she'd just wanted to see how he was doing.

"Oh, well, I'm doing okay, as you can see," said Ferrer for lack of better, smiling thinly, indicating with a vague wave of the hand the breathing tube and the perfusion.

After which nothing more of substance was said between them; she seemed like the sort who speaks little, hovering near the door as if constantly on the point of leaving. Before she did leave, she offered to come back and see how he was doing again, if he wished. He agreed, but as if against his will: deep down, he didn't really give a shit about this girl, couldn't make out the reasons for her visit, didn't understand what it was she wanted from him.

For the three days that Ferrer had to spend in the

intensive care ward, then, the young woman came to visit, always at the same hour of the afternoon, never for more than fifteen minutes at a stretch. The first time, she sat in the heavy armchair with pale and seemingly dirty plastic strips that she pulled close to the bed. Then, having gotten up, she stood for a moment near the window that still framed the distant tree—from which, through the open panes, drifted the song of a bird that briefly made the emerald shimmer and vibrate. And the second and third days, she sat at the foot of the bed that was way too tightly made: the entire time of her visit, Ferrer didn't dare move his wedged extremities, insteps arched, toes curled by the sheet stretched taut as a tent.

But even so, on the third day, before she left, he asked her what her name was. Hélène. Hélène, okay. Not bad, as names go. And what did she do in life? She paused a moment before answering.

25

Meanwhile, Baumgartner is trying to park his automobile in front of a large seaside hotel located in Mimizan-Plage, in the northwest part of the Pyrénées-Atlantiques, on the fringes of the territory that he usually crisscrosses these days. The hotel doesn't look too grand, but it's not easy finding something in this season, and moreover even this establishment is booked up: its vast parking lot disgorges nonnative license plates; Baumgartner was smart to reserve ahead.

He drives slowly, then, up and down the lanes of the parking lot, passing by couples and families dressed in shorts and brightly colored effects, in forced march toward a dip in the ocean. The sun beats down on the panorama, the asphalt is burning, and the barefoot children hop and complain. Every parking spot is taken, none opens up, the whole process drags on; Baumgartner could get exasperated but he has all the time in the world, and looking for a space allows him to occupy this time. He carefully avoids parking his car on places where a mark on the ground, the pictogram of a wheelchair, indicates that they are reserved for the disabled. Not that Baumgartner is especially civic-minded or particularly sensitive to the fate of such persons: no, confusedly it's just a matter of not becoming disabled himself by a backlash of who knows what, the effect of God knows what contagion.

The parking issue finally resolved, Baumgartner pulls his suitcase from the trunk of the Fiat and heads toward the hotel entrance. The facade must have been repainted not so long ago; milky constellations spread discreetly in a few of its corners and the foyer bathes in an odor of whitewash, sour and fresh like curdled milk. Around the building one can still spot a few traces of the recent scaffolding, shreds of dirty plastic stuffed into containers placed in the limbo of the parking lot, planks encrusted with cement haphazardly piled in a hidden corner. Enameled with red blotches on his forehead, the receptionist feverishly scratches his right shoulder while verifying Baumgartner's reservation on his register.

The room is dark and not very inviting; the fragile, wobbly furniture seems fake like theater props, the bed offers a mattress curved in like a hammock, and the dimensions of the drawn curtains do not match those of the window. Above a hard and desperate couch, a crappy lithograph offers up a few zinnias, but Baumgartner pays it no attention: he walks directly to the telephone, dropping his luggage on the way, and dials a number. The line must be busy, since Baumgartner grimaces, hangs up, removes his jacket, and paces around his suitcase without opening it.

Several minutes later, when he goes into the bathroom to wash his hands, the opening and closing of the faucets unleash seismic shock waves in the plumbing throughout the building; then Baumgartner skids on the slippery tiles. Back in his room, he pulls open the curtains and posts himself in front of the window to discover that it overlooks a pit, a dark air shaft, a choking chimney of pitiful diameter with a filthy glassed-in top. It's too much: bathed in sweat, Baumgartner grabs the phone again, calls the reception desk, and demands a room change. Scratching himself, the receptionist gives him the number of the only other available room, one floor above, but no one from the decidedly casual hotel staff comes to take his bags, which he carries up the stairs himself.

And one floor up, the same scene plays out point for point: Baumgartner again tries to telephone but it's still busy. He seems once more on the verge of exasperation but he calms down, opens his suitcase, and arranges his belongings in the tenebrous closet and the pitch-pine chest of drawers. Then he inspects his new room, which is the exact double of the first, save for the lithograph above the sorry couch: crocuses have replaced the zinnias. And if the window looks out indifferently on the parking lot, at least it lets in a little sunlight. At least from there Baumgartner can keep an eye on his car.

26

"Doctor, as a matter of fact, me too," Hélène then answered after a pause, "but not exactly. And anyway, not anymore. I mean, I don't practice anymore." On top of which, she had never treated anyone, disdaining repetitive patients for basic research, which an inheritance then a pension had in any case allowed her to abandon two years ago. Her last position had been at the Salpêtrière, in immunology. "I looked for antibodies, checked to see if there were any, calculated their quality, tried to see what they looked like. I studied their activity, you see?"

"Of course, or at least I think so," hesitated Ferrer, for whom, like Baumgartner, and in keeping with Sarradon's instructions, it was time to change rooms two days later but two floors down.

This new room was fairly similar to the last, but one and a half times as large, since it was made for three beds. It was cluttered up with less medical machinery; the walls this time were pale yellow and the windows looked out not onto a tree but onto a mediocre brick building. Felix Ferrer's neighbors were, to his left, a solid fellow from Ariège, built like a pillar, seemingly in tip-top shape, and about whom Ferrer would never understand what he was doing there; to his right, a skinny Breton who looked like a far-sighted atomic scientist, who kept his face buried in a magazine and was suffering from arrhythmia. It wasn't often that anyone came to visit them: twice the mother of the arrhythmic (inaudible whispered colloquy, no information), once the brother of the Ariégois (very loud commentary on a great ballgame, very little information). The rest of the time, Ferrer's dealings with them were limited to negotiations over the TV channel and volume level.

Though Hélène visited daily, Ferrer continued to act not especially welcoming toward her, didn't show the slightest happiness when she opened the door to his room. Not that he had anything against her, but his thoughts were elsewhere. As of the young woman's first appearance, on the other hand, the roommates had been visibly impressed. Then, in the days that followed, they looked at her each time more covetously, each in his own way—frontal and talkative in Ariège, allusively oblique in the Morbihan. But even his neighbors' appetency did not act mimetically on him, as is sometimes the case. You know what I'm talking about: you don't particularly desire a person, but then a second person, desiring her in your stead, gives you the idea, even the authorization, even the obligation to begin desiring her yourself. Such things happen at times, such things have been seen before; but no, not here; here they were not seen.

At the same time, it can be fairly handy to have someone who wants to take care of you, who can run a few errands, bring you the daily papers unbidden, which you then hand over to the Breton. If flowers had been permitted in the ward, perhaps she'd have brought some of those as well. On each of her visits, Hélène checked on Ferrer's condition, examining the curves and diagrams hanging from the head of his bed with a professional eye, but the terrain of their conversation did not go beyond this clinical horizon. Apart from her former professional activities, she never let slip a single word about her past. The notions evoked earlier of an inheritance and pension, though potentially rich in biographical terms, were never subsequently developed. It never again happened, either, that Ferrer felt any desire to tell her about his life, which these days did not strike him as especially noteworthy or enviable.

At first, then, Hélène came every day as if it were her job, a charitable mission she'd been entrusted with, and when Ferrer began wondering what exactly it was she wanted, he naturally didn't have the nerve to ask. She was neutral and almost cold, and although she seemed perfectly available, she left no openings for anything. All the more so in that availability isn't everything; it doesn't necessarily arouse desire. And in any case, Ferrer, tired, dreading his ruin above all, less afraid of his doctors than of his bankers, found himself in a floating anxiety that was not conducive to seduction. Of course he wasn't blind, of course he saw that Hélène was a beautiful woman, but he always regarded her as if through a bullet-proof, impulse-proof window. Their exchanges were rather abstract or totally concrete, leaving no place for affect, locking down sentiment. It was a little frustrating, and at the same time fairly restful. Soon she must have admitted as much herself, for she began spacing out her visits, coming by only once every two or three days.

Still, at the end of three weeks, when the time came for Ferrer to go home, as promised Hélène offered to handle the formalities. That was on a Tuesday just before noon; Ferrer felt a little weak and unsteady on his legs, standing with his little bag in his hand. She arrived; they took a taxi. And here he was again, incorrigible, despite the silent company of Hélène in the backseat, already starting to look at girls on the street again through the taxi windows until he arrived home, or more precisely in front of his home. Hélène did not come in. But wasn't it the least he could do to invite her for dinner tomorrow or the next day, later that week, I don't know, it seemed the right thing to do. Ferrer thought so. So let's say tomorrow, might as well get it over with as soon as possible, and then we have to think of a restaurant to meet in: after a few hesitations, Ferrer suggested one that had recently opened near Rue du Louvre, right next to Saint-Germain-l'Auxerrois, I don't know if you know it. She knew it. So, tomorrow night, then?

27

But first, the next morning, Ferrer took up his old activities. Elisabeth, who had reopened the gallery two days before, told him of the few things that had happened in his absence: not many arrivals of new works and little mail, no phone messages, not one fax, zero e-mails. Normal stagnation for the off-season. The usual collectors hadn't yet shown their faces. All of them must still have been on vacation, except for Réparaz who had just called to announce his visit and, well well, the door opens and here he is again, old Réparaz, dressed as always in navy blue flannel from head to toe with his little initials embroidered on the pocket of his shirt. A while since we saw him last.

He arrived, shook hands, exclaiming how happy he was with the Martinov he'd bought earlier that year, you remember, the big yellow Martinov.

"Of course," said Ferrer. "Anyway, they're all yellow to some degree."

"And have you gotten in any new pieces since?" worried the businessman.

"Of course," said Ferrer, "a few little things, but I haven't had time to hang them all yet, you understand, I've only just reopened. Most of what's here you've already seen."

"I think I'll take a look around all the same," declared Réparaz.

The collector circled around the gallery with a suspicious look, pushing his glasses up the bridge of his nose or nibbling their stems while walking quickly past most of the works. He finally came to a halt in front of a 60″ × 80″ oil on backed canvas depicting a gang rape, hung earlier that year in a heavy frame made of thick barbed wire. After twenty seconds, Ferrer went to join him.

"I thought this one would appeal to you," he said. "There's something about it, eh?"

"This one, yes, perhaps," Réparaz went pensively. "This one I could easily see hanging in my house. Of course it's a tad big, but what worries me more is the frame. Couldn't we change the frame?"

"Now hold on," said Ferrer. "You can see that the image is a little violent, I mean you agree it's a bit brutal. The artist had that frame made especially for this, you understand, because it's part of the entire picture. It's absolutely part of the picture."

"If you say so," said the collector.

"Obviously," said Ferrer. "And besides, it's not expensive."

"Let me think about it," said Réparaz. "I'll talk to my wife. It's also that the subject, you see, is a bit touchy. Since after all it's a little— I wouldn't want her to—"

"I understand completely," said Ferrer. "Think about it. Talk to her."

After Réparaz left, no one else entered the gallery

until closing time, which he and Elisabeth agreed to move forward. A little later, Ferrer went to meet Hélène at the appointed restaurant, a vast, dark room spangled with small round tables shrouded in white tablecloths, topped with intimate copper lamps and small studied bouquets, where one is lissomely served by beautiful exotic creatures. Ferrer often saw people he knew there without necessarily greeting them, but he always enjoyed chatting up the creatures. In that regard, this evening, manners would dictate that he behave himself even at the cost of being a little bored by Hélène, who was still not overly talkative and was now dressed in a light-gray tailored suit with white pinstripes. If this suit, alas, was not excessively low-cut, Ferrer could nonetheless observe that around the young woman's neck, held by a thin platinum chain, an arrow-shaped pendant clearly indicated which direction her breasts were in: that's something that holds your attention; that's something that keeps you looking.

Whether innocently or by design, Hélène still spoke little, but at least she knew how to listen, to restart her interlocutor with a well-placed monosyllable, skirt around awkward silences by asking just the right question at just the right moment. Constantly redirecting his glance toward the little arrow to buck himself up but definitely without managing, any more than in the hospital, to give birth and substance to any lust for her—and that I really can't figure out, I who am here to tell you that Hélène is highly desirable—Ferrer thus supplied most of the conversation by speaking about his trade: art market (fairly quiet at the moment), current trends (it's a bit complicated, somewhat scattered, one could go back as far as Duchamp, actually), and ongoing debates (as you can well imagine, Hélène, the moment art and money come in contact, sparks inevitably fly), collectors (more and more cautious, which I perfectly understand), artists (less and less engaged, which I completely understand), and models (there aren't any more in the classical sense of the word, which I find totally understandable). Preferring not to make himself look ridiculous, he abstained from relating his journey to the Great North and what had regrettably followed. But, superficial as they were and even though belaboring the obvious, his statements did not seem to bore Hélène, to whom, force of habit, Ferrer suggested going to have a nightcap after dinner.

Now often in such conditions—leaving the restaurant together, last drink—a man who has taken care not to ingest garlic, red cabbage, or too many last drinks tries to kiss a woman. It's the way things are, it's how they're done, and yet, here again, no such thing occurred. And still no way of knowing if Ferrer is intimidated, if he's afraid of rejection, or if it's just that he doesn't give a damn. It is not impossible, Feldman would say—Feldman who started off in psychiatry before shifting to cardiology—not impossible that the heart attack, then the hospitalization, might have provoked a temporary libidinal insufficiency—not a complete psychological breakdown, don't get me wrong, but possibly the source of some minor inhibitions. Libidinal insufficiency my ass, Ferrer would have replied—Ferrer who, shying away from the embrace, nonetheless suggested to Hélène, since all this seemed to interest her, that she come by the gallery one of these days.

The day she came by, at the end of a rainy afternoon, no more petroleum-colored or light-gray suit, nor loose ensemble, just a white blouse and white jeans beneath a slightly overlarge raincoat. They talked for five minutes; Ferrer, still not entirely at ease, commented on a few works for her (a small Beucler and four mounds by Estrellas), then he let her continue touring the gallery on her own. She ignored some smaller pieces by Martinov, spent a lot of time with the photos by Marie-Nicole Guimard, lightly touched one of Schwartz's ventilating fans installed way in back, and barely slowed down in front of the gang rape. Without losing her completely from sight, Ferrer, leaning on his desk, was making a show of going over the layout of the next Martinov catalogue with Elisabeth when, from out of nowhere: Spontini. "Ah, Spontini," Ferrer said gaily. "How are the temperas coming?"

From the rear of the gallery, Hélène gathered that the aforementioned Spontini had not come to present his works, neither tempera nor anything else, but his grievances. The word *contract* was uttered. The term *endorsement* was invoked. Percentages were disputed. Too far away to follow the conversation, Hélène suddenly appeared to take an interest in some recent Blaviers hanging behind the desk.

"You understand that *I*," said Ferrer, "have a certain sense of my job, and I believe that it's worth fifty percent of the work. And if *you* now figure that it's worth forty, for example, we're not going to see eye to eye."

"I think that's too much," said Spontini, "I think that's enormous. I really think that's enormous. It's off the charts. If you want to know the truth, I sometimes wonder if I wouldn't be better off with Abitbol. He's only waiting for me to say the word, Abitbol, I saw him again the other day at the Castagnier opening."

"Anyway," said Ferrer wearily, "this isn't the first time you've tried to pull this shit. For ten years you've taken advantage of working with me to meet everyone who's anyone and you've sold things behind my back while you were still exhibiting here, and don't think I don't know it. So mark my words, if you want to pull this kind of shit, Abitbol or no Abitbol, the door is that way. I mean, do you have any idea how tough the work situation is in France these days?"

"But," Spontini pointed out, "look at Beucler. After everything he's done to you, he's still here all the same."

"Beucler is a different matter," said Ferrer. "Beucler is a special case."

"Yeah, but even so," Spontini insisted. "He's scamming you with a vengeance. He leaves you a ten-percent commission, Beucler, while he pockets ninety and everyone in the business knows it. And after all that he's still here, and you're even working out a deal for him in Japan. I've heard about it, I know all about that one, too, everybody knows about it."

"Beucler is a special case," Ferrer repeated, "and that's all there is to it. I admit I thought about firing him, but he's still here. It's no more rational than that. Let's drop the subject, if you don't mind."

Fresh out of arguments, soon they were no longer speaking at all. Spontini left, muttering complaints filigreed with threats; Ferrer, riddled with fatigue, let himself collapse into a chair; Hélène, back to see the Schwartz, smiled at him from across the room. He gave her back a tight grimace while getting up, then, coming toward her: "You heard that, I imagine you understood what it was about. You must think I'm a monster."

"No, no," said Hélène.

"I hate that kind of situation," Ferrer commented, massaging his cheeks. "It's the worst part of this business. I so wish I could delegate those things to someone else. I used to have an assistant, Delahaye, I told you about him. He was starting to get good at handling those things for me and then the asshole had to go and die. It's too bad, because Delahaye was good, he was really good at this kind of situation."

He was massaging his temples now. He looked tired.

"You know," Hélène said, "I don't have a lot to do these days. I could help you out, if you want."

"That's very kind of you," Ferrer smiled sadly, "but I really can't accept. Just between you and me, in our current spot, I couldn't even pay you."

"Are things that bad?" she said.

"I've run into some bad luck lately," Ferrer admitted. "I'll tell you about it."

I'm Gone

So he told. Everything. From the beginning. When he had finished the tale of his misadventures, night had fallen. Outside, in the heights of the construction site, the two yellow cranes blinked from the ends of their jibs, while in the sky flew the Paris-Singapore, blinking at the same rhythm from the tips of its wings. Thus, addressing synchronic winks to each other between earth and sky, they mutually signaled their presence.

28

Personally, I've had it up to here with Baumgartner. His daily life is too boring. Apart from living in a hotel, telephoning every other day, and visiting whatever falls in his sights, he really doesn't do much. The whole thing lacks motivation. Since leaving Paris for the southwest, he's spent his time meandering around behind the wheel of his white Fiat, a simple vehicle without options or ornaments, with nothing stuck to the windows or suspended from the rearview mirror. He mostly takes the local highways. One morning, a Sunday, he arrives in Biarritz.

As the ocean is strong and heaving mightily, and as it's a warm and hazy Sunday, the inhabitants of Biarritz have come out to watch the waves. They stand in rows on several tiers, along the beaches but also on terraces, jetties, balconies, knolls, and walkways that overlook the muscular ocean; they are lined up along every vantage point, watching it run through its furious performance. This spectacle stupefies man and paralyzes him; he can contemplate it indefinitely without ever tiring, with no reason to stop. Fire also has this effect; rain sometimes has this effect; the flow of passersby from a sidewalk table can have it, too.

In Biarritz this Sunday, near the lighthouse, Baumgartner sees a young man venture near the ocean, at the far edge of a rocky promontory, risking getting himself soaked through by sprays of nervous foam, which he sidesteps with a torero's sway. Moreover, it's in bull-fighting terms that he comments on the prowess of the successive waves, salutes (*Olé*) an especially scenic burst, invites (*Toro toro*) a promising, rumbling swell (*Torito bueno*)—all encouragements, calls, and expressions that are addressed to the beasts in the ring. Then after the wave has savagely dashed in every direction, dislocated itself in explosions, when this watery monster has come to lie down and die at his feet, the young man, arm outstretched and hand raised as if to immobilize time, addresses it with the gesture of matadors in the interval after the *estocada*, sometimes a bit long, in which the animal remains standing while the life drains out of him, until he collapses, often to the side and perpendicular to his stiffened hooves.

Baumgartner does not spend more than two days in Biarritz, just enough time for the ocean to catch its breath, then he heads off toward the interior lands. Even more than during his earlier trip, Baumgartner does not linger in cities, which he only crosses through or skirts around via their byroads whenever possible. He'd rather stop in a village, sit in a café without talking to anyone.

He'd rather listen to people's conversations (*four idle men compare their weights in kilos and each picks the name for himself of the* département *with the matching postal code; the thinnest one, then, declares himself the Meuse [55], the more-or-less normal one takes Les Yvelines [78], the fairly stocky one admits pushing the Territoire de Belfort [90], and the fattest surpasses the Val d'Oise [95]*); read the posters scotch-taped to the mirrors (*LARGE VEGETABLE CONTEST: 8–11, Registration of Vegetables. 11–12:30, Jury Deliberations. 5 pm, Awarding of Prizes and Wine Reception. Eligible for Entry: Leeks, Lettuce, White Cabbage, Brussels Sprouts, Cauliflower, Red Cabbage, Tomatoes, Melons, Pumpkins, Peppers, Zucchini, Red Beets, Carrots, Celery Root, Swiss Chard & Kohlrabi, Turnips & Rape, Winter Radish, Potatoes, Parsnips, Corn, Garlic, Onions. Contest open to all gardeners. Maximum nine vegetables per gardener. One specimen per vegetable. Presented with leaves, stalks & roots if possible. Vegetables will be judged on weight and appearance*); or consult the weather report in the local newspaper (*Rain and storms against a chaotic sky, sometimes accompanied by thunder in the afternoon*).

The weather indeed turns bad, yet Baumgartner is less demanding about the quality of the hotels he patronizes. The establishments he spends his nights in are more basic than ever; it all matters little to him. The first days he never failed to buy the local and national dailies, reading carefully through the Arts and Society pages without ever finding the slightest mention of an antiques theft. When it became clear that no mention was forthcoming, Baumgartner lowered his consumption of press, which he ended up only leafing through distractedly over breakfast, greasing the pages with butter and jam, underlining passages in coffee, creating interlaced circles of orange juice up and down the salmon-colored financial supplement.

One evening under pouring rain, between Auch and Toulouse, he drives through the night that has begun falling earlier and earlier. Beyond the windshield wipers running at top speed, his headlights are barely enough to light the road: he notices only at the last moment, to his right, slightly below the roadway, a silhouette moving along the shoulder. Engulfed in water and darkness, on the point of dissolving in it like a sugar cube, the silhouette does not wave its hand nor even turn around at the approaching cars whose headlights and engines, in any case, are smothered by the storm. If Baumgartner decides to stop, it's less from charity than from reflex, or because he's a little bored; he flicks his blinkers to the right, brakes one hundred yards farther on, and waits for the silhouette to join him.

But it does not quicken its pace, as if it did not draw any causal connection between itself and the stopping of the Fiat. When the figure arrives next to the vehicle, Baumgartner can vaguely make it out through the streaming window: a young woman, it appears, a girl who opens the door and gets in without them exchanging the usual preliminary words between hitchhiker and driver. She tosses her bag onto the backseat and sits down without a word, carefully shutting the door. She is so completely soaked that immediately the windshield is coated in a light mist—Baumgartner sourly imagines the state of the front seat after her passage. Not only is she drenched, she also looks fairly dirty and detached from the world. "Are you making for Toulouse?" Baumgartner asks.

The young lady does not answer immediately; her face in the shadows is not very distinct. Then she utters in a monotonous and recitative voice, a little mechanical and vaguely frightening, that she is not making for Toulouse but going to Toulouse, that it is deplorable and odd that people confuse those two expressions, which nothing justifies, and which in any case is indicative of a general tendency toward linguistic sloppiness that one can only protest, that she in any case strongly protests, and with that she rolls her sopping hair against the headrest and falls asleep. She seems completely deranged.

Baumgartner remains agape and slightly annoyed for a few seconds, then he gently shifts into first as if he were reconsidering before starting up. Five hundred yards later, as the girl begins softly snoring, he is seized by an irritation that nearly makes him pull over and send her back to her liquid obscurity, but he gets hold of himself: she is sleeping peacefully now, her entire relaxed body is in peace, gently held in place by the safety belt; it would not be worthy of the gentleman he has decided to become. This feeling flatters him, but it's mainly something else that holds him back: it's mainly that her voice reminds him of someone. Absorbed by driving through hostile territory, he has few opportunities to glance over at her, and in any case the woman is leaning on the window with her back to him. But in a flash Baumgartner recognizes her, realizes her identity; it's totally implausible but there you have it. All

the way to Toulouse he drives on eggshells, holding his
breath and avoiding the slightest pothole, the least jolt
that might wake her. The trip lasts no less than an hour.

Arriving in Toulouse in the middle of the night,
Baumgartner lets the girl out in front of the station
without putting on the overhead light, facing in the
other direction while she undoes her seat belt and
gets out, thanking him almost inaudibly, twice. Before
starting up again, Baumgartner watches her walk away
toward the station cafeteria in the rearview mirror,
never turning back. Since it's dark, and since that girl
(who, if you ask me, is plumb crazy) barely looked at
him, we have every reason to believe that she hasn't
identified him, or at least so he fervently hopes.

Over the next few days, Baumgartner pursues his
rambling itinerary. He gets to know the melancholy of
roadside restaurants, the acrid awakenings in as-yet-
unheated hotel rooms, the numbness of rural zones
and construction sites, the bitterness of impossible af-
finities. It lasts for another two weeks or so, until mid-
September, at which point he finally notices that he's
being followed.

29

During those same two weeks, Hélène continued to visit the gallery fairly often. As at the hospital, she dropped in at odd times but never stayed for more than an hour, once every two or three days, and as at the hospital Ferrer greeted her politely but stiffly, his attentions too courteous and his smiles a bit forced, as if he were humoring a fragile relative.

In the end, the long tale he'd told her of his recent woes hadn't really brought them much closer. She had listened without any particular reaction, neither admiration at Ferrer's northern exploits nor commiseration, even laughter, at the dismaying conclusion of the affair. And if she hadn't renewed her offer to help around the gallery, clearly it wasn't for financial reasons. Be that as it may, the situation hadn't progressed too far; they still looked for things to say to each other without always finding them, which sometimes produced silences. That might not have been so bad; silence can sometimes be a good thing. Combined with the proper glance and smile, silence can yield excellent results, rare intensities, subtle perspectives, exquisite aftertastes, definitive decisions. But here, no: there was only a pasty, heavy muteness, cumbersome like sticky tar on the sole of your shoe. After a while, they couldn't stand it anymore. Hélène started coming by less and less often, then hardly at all.

At first Ferrer had been relieved, naturally, but also naturally it soon created a little void that he hadn't expected. He found himself waiting for her, glancing oh so casually down the street, and it goes without saying that she'd never given him her address or left any kind of telephone number, since idiot Ferrer had never thought to ask. And now it was a Monday morning, which is never a great thing. Shuttered shops, cloudy sky, opaque air, dirty sidewalks: in short, everything was closed in every direction. It was as depressing as a Sunday, without the alibi of having nothing to do. Scattered little clusters of pedestrians crossed the streets off the zebra stripes toward the only market on duty, and Ferrer's mood was the same rancid yellow as the cranes in the construction site across the way and the electric sign of the supermarket. It was the wrong moment for Spontini to reappear, bent on reiterating his dissatisfaction with percentages.

He was not given time to make much of an argument: "Listen," Ferrer interrupted, "I'm going to tell you what I really think, now. You don't work enough, frankly your work hasn't evolved. Strictly between us, what you're doing now doesn't interest me all that much, get it?"

"What does that mean?" worried Spontini.

"It means that just because you've sold to two art centers and three private collectors, you still don't qualify as an artist," said Ferrer. "As far as I'm concerned, you're nothing. Wait until you have regular collectors abroad, then you can talk about a career. It also means that if you're not happy, the door is right there."

In the frame of that door, as he left the gallery, Spontini nearly ran into a guy of about thirty wearing blue jeans and a leather jacket, which these days doesn't make you look like an artist, and still less a collector, but rather a young police detective, and in fact that's just what the man was.

"You remember me," said Supin. "I'm from Criminal Records. I'm here about your case."

Without going into the technical details, the situation according to Supin was as follows: Good news and bad news, I'd rather start with the bad, which is that the electron microscope analysis of samples lifted from the studio had told them nothing. On the other hand, the good news was that in the pocket of a thawed corpse, discovered by chance and imperfectly preserved, they had found among old, stiff, crumpled Kleenexes, compact as flat stones or cakes of soap in the final stages of their career, a scrap of paper bearing a license number. Once they'd identified the registration, certain cross-checks allowed them to posit that the Fiat in question had some involvement in the theft reported by Ferrer. So they were looking for it. That's where things stood.

This immediately put Ferrer in a better mood. Before shutting the gallery, at the close of the afternoon, he was visited by a young artist named Corday. The latter presented projects, sketches, mock-ups, and manufacturing invoices. He did not, unfortunately, have the funds necessary to achieve all his objectives. ·

"But this is good," said Ferrer, "it's very good, I like it a lot. Tell you what, we'll mount an exhibition."

"No!" went the other.

"Yes, yes, sure," said Ferrer, "of course, of course we will. And if that one works out, we'll do another."

"So, are we going to sign a contract?" the other imagined.

"Easy," said Ferrer, "take it easy. Contracts don't get signed just like that. Come back and see me the day after tomorrow."

30

Having gone into effect in 1995, the Schengen Agreement inaugurated, as everyone knows, the unrestricted circulation of persons between the member countries of Europe. The abolition of interior border controls, along with reinforced surveillance at the external frontiers, authorizes the rich to visit the rich, comfortably among their own kind, opening their arms wide the better to shut them to the poor, who, even more inbred, understand their pain all the better. Naturally the customs institutions remain, and although the civilian may still not smuggle whatever he wants with impunity, he can at least move around now without waiting an hour at the border for someone to sniff his passport. This is what Baumgartner is getting ready to do.

By dint of having crisscrossed the area, the humblest eco-museums, curiosities, scenic views, and rest stops situated in the lower left-hand corner of the French map hold no more secrets for him. Of late he hasn't ventured away from the extreme southwest tip, never more than an hour from the border, as if, a semiclandestine passenger aboard a leaky steamship, he were always hovering near the lifeboats, hidden behind a ventilator.

But Baumgartner didn't need to notice more than three times in three days the same red-clad, red-helmeted motorcyclist to decide on a change of scenery. This individual first appeared to him in the rearview mirror, some distance back, on a winding local highway in the open mountain range, emerging and eclipsing with the hairpin turns. Another time, at a toll booth, not far from two motorcycle cops in black, it seemed that the same person was leaning on his bike and biting into a sandwich—evidently the helmet didn't inhibit the vertical motion of his jaws. The third time, apparently broken down on the side of a local highway under the renewed rain, the man was hanging on to an emergency phone: coming up the roadside, Baumgartner aimed the right tires of his car toward a deep, wide puddle. He laughed to watch, in his mirror, the man jump under the muddy spray, and was even a little disappointed not to see him shake his fist.

Baumgartner's life, which these past weeks had been fairly loose-ended, silent, muffled like a bad fog, now experienced a little animation with the advent of the red cyclist. The other's presence and the concern it inspired made him feel less alone, attenuating the echo produced, in hotel rooms, by each of his movements. The daily calls to Paris, his only remaining connection to the world, blunted his isolation; it was moreover by telephone that he announced his departure for Spain. And besides, he said, autumn was here, the evenings were getting chilly. It's simple, it rains all the time. I'll be better off down there.

From where he is, i.e, today, Thursday morning, in Saint-Jean-de-Luz, there are two possible roads to Spain. Either Autoroute 63, where the border consists in aligned arches and columns, punctuated by road signs and emblems; old yellowish heat-sealed spots peeling off the asphalt; closed, abandoned booths, their barriers perpetually raised on three scattered, idle functionaries wearing indifferent uniforms, turning their backs to the traffic and wondering what the hell they're doing there. Or you can take the old Highway 10: this is what Baumgartner chooses.

On Highway 10, it's at Béhobie that you cross the border, which is embodied by a bridge over the Bidasoa. Enormous trucks are parked in front of the last French building, a bank, and customs on the other side now consists in desolate, vandalized blockhouses, their caved-in shutters askew. The remains of their dirty windows poorly conceal the rubble and detritus cluttering them up and the whole thing is very sad, but they're going to be torn down soon: given the state of the installations, the Madrid authorities have endorsed the procedure initiated by the community; it's only a matter of time. The steam shovels are chomping at the bit and everyone is waiting for the official clearance, at which point they can sign the permit that will let them blow the whole thing sky high.

The entire area, moreover, already looks like a demolition yard. A number of houses with fallen walls have been invaded by parasitic vegetation that has grown inordinately through the collapsed roofs. The more recent constructions, not yet ripe, have various textiles and blackish plastics flapping from their windows. It smells of sour rust, and the sky, too, is the color of rust or excrement, barely distinguishable behind the carbon of the rain. Several factories look like they've been destroyed even before the bankruptcy petition was filed, surrounded by heaps of garbage, marked by deserted scaffolds and slathered with graffiti. Past the bridge, the haphazardly parked vehicles await their drivers, who have gotten out to buy duty-free alcohol and tobacco. Then, once they've left, the road choked by red lights convulses in a chronic bottleneck: they progress in spasms like a cough.

Like everyone else, Baumgartner gets out of the car and runs in the rain toward the discount shops, the collar of his raincoat pulled up over his skull. One shop is selling small black nylon rain hats with plaid lining for thirty-five francs, a lucky break. Baumgartner tries several on. Size 58 is too small, 60 is a bit large, so he buys without hesitation or trial a 59, which must be right, but which, after he looks at it in the makeup mirror of his car, somehow doesn't seem to fit right either—too late and too bad. The Fiat crosses the border without incident, and Baumgartner breathes easier afterward.

Your body changes when crossing a border—everyone knows this, too—your eyes change lens and focal depth, the air modifies its density, and scents and sounds particularly stand out; even the sun wears a different face. Rusts corrode the road signs in unknown ways, while the signs themselves announce an innovative conception of steep inclines, bends in the road, or reduced speed ahead. Some of these signs remain obscure, moreover, and Baumgartner feels himself becoming someone else, or rather the same and

someone else at once, as if he's had all his blood trans-
fused. On top of which, the minute he crosses the border, a soft breeze unfamiliar to France starts blowing.

Two miles past the former border post, a new traffic
jam forms. A van with the word *Policia* blocks the
road in the opposite direction. Men in black uniforms
filter the traffic, and fifty yards beyond that, their
chests barred by diagonal machine-pistols, others in
camouflage watch the embankment. Baumgartner does
not feel especially concerned but, two miles farther on,
as he's rolling along at moderate speed, a navy blue
Renault van passes him. Instead of cutting in front, the
van pulls alongside, then an arm emerges from a lowered window, in a rolled-up sleeve of the same color
and extended by a long pale hand whose slender fingers wave slowly up and down, tap the air in cadence,
beat time while lithely indicating the shoulder of the
road onto which, calmly but firmly, Baumgartner's car
is forced to pull over.

Baumgartner activates his blinker while exhorting
himself not to sweat, brakes slowly, then stops. Once
the blue van has come to a gentle halt a dozen yards
ahead of the Fiat, two men get out. They are Spanish
border guards, smiling and clean-shaven; their hair
has retained all the grooves of the comb, their uniforms
are well starched, a song still plays about their lips as
they approach Baumgartner with a dancing step. One
speaks almost accentless French, the other keeps silent.
"Mobile Customs, Sir," says the one who speaks, "just
a little formality. Car registration and identity papers
and please be so good as to open your trunk."

It takes less than a minute for the contents of the trunk, inspected by the silent one, to reveal themselves of no interest: suitcase, change of clothes, toiletries. The speechless customs man closes it with a watchmaker's delicacy while the other, Baumgartner's identity in hand, heads on tiptoe toward the van from which he reemerges three minutes later, no doubt having phoned in or consulted a screen. "Very good, Sir," he says. "Kindly accept our deepest apologies and our gratitude for your cooperation, which does us honor and reinforces our inalterable respect for the fundamental morality that is indissociable from the mission we have by good fortune been entrusted and to which we devote our lives absolutely and without distractions even of a familial nature (Yes, says Baumgartner) whatever the obstacles whose very size and brutality inspire and enhance the impetus which daily moves us to battle the cancer that is violation of the principles of municipal taxation (Yes, yes, says Baumgartner) but which also allows me to wish you among many other things, in the name of my people as a whole and of our customs institution in particular, an excellent journey."

"Thank you, thank you," says Baumgartner, his head swimming; then he shifts into the wrong gear and stalls, but finally drives off.

He is back on the road now. Autumn has indeed arrived, is even fairly well advanced, since right now the sky is crossed by a flock of storks following the highway axis. These storks are migrating; it's the season; they're doing their yearly Potsdam-Nouakchott via Gibraltar almost without stopping, tracing the paths of existing roads. They will stop only once, practically at midway, on the interminable straight line that runs unbroken from Algeciras to Málaga; the road is lined with pylons atop which the wise authorities have thought to install vast stork-sized nests. There they will take some rest, time to breathe a little, cackle among themselves awhile, massacre native rats and vipers, maybe even a nice little carcass, you never know—while upstream the two good-looking Spanish customs men glance at each other and burst out laughing. "*Me parece, tío*," says the man who talks to the one who doesn't, "*que hemos dado tiempo al Tiempo*." They both double over; the breeze turns cooler.

And twenty minutes later, a little before noon, Baumgartner enters a seaside resort town. He parks his Fiat in the underground lot in the center, takes a room at the London & England Hotel, which looks out on the bay, then goes out again to wander a moment, with no particular goal, around the clear wide streets of the central quarter with its purveyors of luxury and other garments. He knows enough Spanish to try on a pair of trousers in a shop, but not enough to explain why he doesn't want them. Then he returns to the old town where the streets harbor a supernatural multitude of bars. Entering one of them, Baumgartner points to some little poached or grilled things in sauce displayed on the counter, which he devours quickly while standing; then he returns to the hotel via the promenade along the bay.

And two weeks later it turns quite cold for early October. On the promenade, everyone is already dressed in parkas and overcoats, furs and scarves; quilts smother baby carriages that are pushed more briskly. From the window of his room in the London & England Hotel, Baumgartner sees a woman with the magnificent physique of a sea lion, wearing a black one-piece bathing suit, enter the verdigris ocean whose color alone gives you the chills. She is absolutely alone in the bay, under a brownish-gray sky that doesn't make it feel any warmer; people on the promenade stop to watch. She moves forward into the icy water until it reaches her ankles, her knees, her pubis, then her waist, at which point, before plunging in with outstretched arms, she crosses herself, and Baumgartner envies her. What has she got that I haven't to be able to do that? Maybe it's just that she knows how to swim. I don't. I know the sign of the cross, but how to swim, no.

"So are we drawing up this contract or what?" Corday feverishly insisted the next morning.

"The contract, the contract," mused Ferrer, already less enthusiastic than the day before, "not right away. For the moment, let's just say that I'll take care of manufacturing the works, okay? I'll take over that whole side of it. And I'll reimburse myself from the proceeds when they sell. Then we'll have to see if the stuff catches on, if we can find you another place to exhibit. Belgium or Germany, something like that. If it doesn't catch on, we'll stay mostly in France, try to find something in a cultural center, for instance. Then afterward we'll try to get a piece bought by some department store or other, you know, then we can get that piece shown somewhere, that would already create a little momentum. And after that, New York."

"New York!" the other gawped in echo.

"New York," repeated Ferrer, "New York. It's always pretty much the same scenario, you see? Then if all that works out, we can put whatever we want in the contract, at that point. Would you excuse me a moment?"

Near the entrance, pondering a recent work, a giant asbestos bra by the husband of the lover of Schwartz who had recommended it to Ferrer, stood Criminal

Investigations officer Supin. He looked so young; he was still wearing his standard cool young cop outfit, an outfit he profoundly disliked, but a job's a job. He mainly seemed happy to be there, Ferrer gallery, modern art, finally something he could relate to.

"About that Fiat," said Supin. "I just wanted to let you know we think we've spotted it near the Spanish border. Mobile Customs, routine check—a lucky break. They tried to detain the driver for a while, but of course customs can't do much in matters like this. They tipped us off right away, we're lucky we get along so well with our counterparts in the sector. Obviously I'm going to try to locate the individual. I've got some colleagues down there who I'll put on the case, but I can't guarantee anything. If I find something out I'll call you. I'll let you know what's what tonight or tomorrow, in any case. Tell me, just out of curiosity, how much does that kind of thing go for, that big bra over there?"

After Supin went reeling out, floored by the price, and despite his hopeful information, a somber melancholy flooded Ferrer. He had gotten rid of Corday as expeditiously as possible, no longer sure of being able to keep even his minimal promises; we'd see. He had to force himself not to let this black abyss swallow everything, especially not infect his professional life and his views on art in general. Casting a panoramic and suddenly disgusted glance over the works exhibited in his gallery, he was invaded by doubt and again had to close up earlier than usual. He let Elisabeth go for the day before locking the glass door and electrically lowering the iron shutter, then walked, hunched against the violent wind that was blowing, up to the Saint-Lazare metro station. Transfer at Opéra, get out at Châtelet; the courthouse was just across the Seine, less than a two-minute walk from there. Ferrer's various professional and financial troubles were not the only source of his depression, his hunched back and pinched face: it's also that it was October 10, and going somewhere to get divorced is never an enticing prospect.

He was, of course, not the only one in this situation, which was no consolation: the waiting room was filled with couples at the end of their journey. Some didn't seem to get along too badly despite the circumstances, chatting quietly with their attorneys. The summons was for eleven-thirty and, at forty past, Suzanne still hadn't arrived—always late, Ferrer said to himself with a trace memory of annoyance, but the family court judge was, too. The waiting room was furnished with uncomfortable plastic chairs attached to the four walls, surrounding a low table covered with a collection of heterogeneous and worn-out publications: legal periodicals, art and health magazines, weeklies consecrated to the lives of celebrities. Ferrer picked one of them up and started leafing through it: as usual, it was composed of photographs of stars, stars of every stripe stemming from the lyrical, televisual, cinematographic, athletic, political, and even culinary spheres. A two-page spread in the centerfold offered up the photo of a superstar flanked by her new conquest, in the background of which, a little out of focus but still perfectly recognizable, one could make out Baumgartner. In four seconds Ferrer would come across that page and that photo, three seconds, two seconds, one second, but Suzanne chose that instant to burst in, and he closed the magazine without regrets.

The judge was a gray-haired woman, at once calm and tense: calm in that she felt accustomed to being a judge, tense in that she knew she would never entirely be accustomed to it. Although she was visibly making an effort to remain cool, Ferrer imagined her as a caring person in her private life, reassuring and perhaps even loving, yes, certainly a good wife and mother though not always a barrel of laughs. Her husband was probably a court clerk who took care of the household chores when she had to be late for dinner, during which they would discuss the fine points of civil jurisprudence. As she first saw the couple together, Ferrer, deeming that her questions didn't apply to him, reacted *a minima*. Suzanne also remained reserved, answering only when she had to and with a distinct economy of means.

"No, no," said Ferrer when the judge confirmed as a formality that there were no children.

"So you've made your decision," said the judge, looking at Suzanne—and, turning to Ferrer: "The husband looks a little less certain than the wife."

"No, yes," Ferrer sputtered. "No problem."

Then she saw each of them individually, one after the other, the wife first. While awaiting his turn, Ferrer did not pick up the same magazine and, when Suzanne came out of the judge's chamber, he stood up and sought her out with a look that she didn't return. He banged against a chair as he headed for the chamber. "Are you absolutely sure you want a divorce?" asked the judge.

"Yes, yes," answered Ferrer.

"Fine," she said, closing the file, and there you had it, it was done.

As they were leaving, Ferrer would gladly have offered to buy Suzanne lunch or just a drink, across the street, for instance, at the Courthouse Brasserie, but she didn't leave him time. Ferrer shuddered, expecting the worst, the humiliating insults and categorical demands he'd managed to avoid in January, but no, no. Simply raising a finger to keep him silent, she opened her bag from which she pulled a spare set of keys to the gallery that had remained behind in Issy, handed them to him without a word, then walked off toward the Pont Saint-Michel to the south. Five motionless seconds later, Ferrer started off toward the Pont au Change to the north.

Later that afternoon, back at the gallery, Ferrer closed up as he did every day at seven o'clock. Night would soon fall; the sun was no longer visible from that part of the Earth. There remained only a pure blue-gray sky, in the middle of which a distant airplane, gathering the last imperceptible rays from below, traced a bright pink line. Again Ferrer stood motionless for a few seconds, gazing down the street before heading off. Like him, the neighborhood shopkeepers were pulling down their iron curtains. The workmen from the construction site across the way had also left work, after prudently setting the jib of the cranes in the direction of the wind for the night. On the facade of the neighboring tall building, every other window was obstructed by parabolic antennas: when the sun was out, these parabolas must have kept it from entering, welcoming in its stead images destined for the television that thus replaced the view.

He was about to walk away from the gallery when a woman's silhouette appeared at the end of the street; her outline was familiar, but it took him a moment to recognize Hélène. It was not the first time Ferrer had some difficulty identifying her: at the hospital, when she came into his room, he experienced the same latency period, knowing perfectly well it was she while each time having to reconstruct her person, go back to square one, as if her features did not spontaneously organize themselves. These features were nonetheless beautiful and harmoniously arranged; that wasn't the problem, and Ferrer could admire each one individually. It was their relationship to each other that was constantly altering, never ending up at exactly the same face. You might have thought they were in perpetual displacement, in precarious balance, as if their very composition were unstable. It was therefore not entirely the same person that Ferrer had before him each time he saw Hélène.

The latter had come by chance, not planning or expecting anything: offering her a drink, Ferrer reopened the gallery. Then, going to fetch some chilled champagne in the studio, he decided to study Hélène's face this time with patience and precision, the way one learns a lesson; to know it once and for all and rid himself of the disturbance it caused. But his efforts were all the more vain in that Hélène today, for the first time, had put on makeup, which changed and complicated everything.

For makeup masks the sensory organs even as it decorates them—or at least, nota bene, those with multiple uses. The mouth, for example—which breathes and speaks and eats, drinks, smiles, whispers, kisses, sucks, licks, bites, pants, sighs, cries, smokes, grimaces, laughs, sings, whistles, hiccups, spits, belches, vomits, exhales—is painted (and that's the least of it) to honor it for carrying out so many noble functions. One can also paint the area around the eyes, which gaze, express, cry, and shut in sleep—equally noble. And one can paint the nails, which have a box seat at the immense and noble variety of manual operations.

But one doesn't put makeup on things that render only one or two services. Neither the ear, good only for hearing, from which one merely dangles a pendant of some kind. Nor the nose—limited to breathing, smelling, and sometimes getting stuffy—which, like ears, might have a hoop attached, or a precious stone, a pearl, or even in certain latitudes a real bone, whereas here one mainly just powders it. But Hélène sported none of these accessories: she had put on just some ruby-colored lipstick, eye shadow hovering somewhere around raw sienna, and a brief shot of eyeliner. As Ferrer saw it, opening the champagne, this would make matters supremely complicated.

Then again, no, it wouldn't have time to make them anything at all, for at that instant the telephone rang:

"Supin here. I'm calling earlier than expected. I think I might have found something." Scrambling for a pencil, Ferrer listened carefully, jotted down a few words on the back of an envelope, then profusely thanked the man from Criminal Records. "It's nothing," said Supin. "Just luck. We have good relations with Spanish customs," he reiterated, "and I have an excellent colleague in the motorcycle cops down there who did a little tailing in his spare time. So much for all that hype about rivalries among the police."

Once he'd hung up, Ferrer nervously filled two champagne flutes, causing them to spill over. "I'm going to have to leave in just a moment," he said. "But in the meantime, maybe we'll finally have something to drink to, you and I."

32

Whether it's by the autoroute or the national highway that you head for the south of Spain, whether you cross the border at Hendaye or Béhobie, you must pass through San Sebastián. After Ferrer had driven through somber industrial wastelands, skirted oppressive blocks of Francoist architecture, and asked himself numerous times what he was doing there, he suddenly entered the large, unexpected seaside resort. It was built on a narrow strip of earth, on either side of a river and a mountain that separated two nearly symmetrical bays, this double indentation tracing an approximate omega, a woman's bust that pushed into the inland regions, two oceanic breasts corseted by the Spanish coast.

Ferrer parked his rental car in the underground lot near the main bay, then registered in a small hotel in the center of town. For a week he walked down wide, calm, airy boulevards, attentively washed, lined with serious, light-colored buildings; but also down short, narrow streets, also swept with care, dark and overhung with narrow, nervous buildings. Palaces and grand hotels, bridges and parks, baroque, gothic, and neogothic churches, spanking new arenas, huge beaches flanked by a thalassotherapy institute, the Royal Tennis Club, and the casino. One more solemn than the next, the four bridges were paved with mosaic tiles and laced with stone, glass, and cast iron, decorated with white and gold obelisks, wrought-iron streetlamps, sphinxes, and turrets bearing royal monograms. The water of the river was green veering to blue as it threw itself into the ocean. Ferrer haunted these bridges, but more often he strode up the promenade that trimmed the conchoidal bay, the center of which was occupied by a little island topped with a minuscule castle.

For days on end he wandered around like this, with no particular goal other than a chance encounter, trying to inventory all the different neighborhoods. He ended up tiring of this city that was both too large and too small, where you were never sure where you were even while knowing it all too well. Supin had given no further indication other than the name San Sebastián, accompanied by a hypothesis with limited probability. Whether the antiques thief was actually living there was anybody's guess.

At mealtimes, Ferrer mainly frequented the many bustling small bars of the old town where you can eat all sorts of things while standing at the counter and where you're not obliged to take your solitary nourishment seated at a table, which can be so demoralizing. But this, too, grew tiring: Ferrer finally came across an unpretentious restaurant near the port where his solitude was less of a burden. He called Elisabeth at the gallery every afternoon, and at night he went to bed early. Still, after a week his undertaking struck him as hopeless. Looking for a stranger in a strange town made no sense at all, and discouragement overtook him. Before thinking about returning to Paris, Ferrer would spend a few more days in this city, but without crisscrossing it in vain, preferring to doze away his afternoons in a deck chair on the beach when the autumn weather allowed, then to kill his last evenings alone at the bar of the María Cristina Hotel in a leather armchair, facing a glass of txakoli and a full-length portrait of a doge.

One evening, when the entire ground floor of the María Cristina was invaded by a noisy party of conventioning oncologists, Ferrer decided to go instead to the London & England Hotel, an establishment only slightly less tony than his, whose bar had the advantage of large airy windows overlooking the bay. The ambience that evening was much calmer than at the María Cristina: three or four middle-aged couples sitting in the common room, two or three men standing alone at the bar, little movement, few comings or goings. Ferrer sat all the way at the end of the room, near one of the large windows. Night had fallen. The lights of the coast were reflected in wavy columns on an ocean of oil, where twenty-five light-colored silhouettes of pleasure craft rested in peace near the port.

Now depending on how your eyes focused on them, these windows allowed you to see either outside or into the immobile common room by a rearview effect. A movement soon appeared at the opposite end of the bar: the revolving door turned on itself for a moment, disgorging Baumgartner, who went to lean against the bar next to the single men, his back turned to the bay. Distantly reflected in the window, those shoulders and that back put a crease in Ferrer's brow. His eyes gradually focused more and more closely on them, then he finally stood up from his seat and approached the bar with a cautious step. Stopping six feet away from Baumgartner, he hesitated a moment, then went closer.

"Excuse me," he said, lightly posing two fingers on the man's shoulder, causing him to turn around. "Well," said Ferrer. "Delahaye. I thought as much."

33

Not content with not being dead, which in the end didn't surprise Ferrer all that much, Delahaye had undergone quite a change in the past few months. He had even been transformed. The jumble of vague and obtuse angles that had always defined his person had given way to a series of razor-sharp lines and perspectives, as if the whole picture had been overly focused.

Now, as Baumgartner, everything about him was impeccably drawn: his tie whose knot (when he wore one) had hung askew at some vague angle from the collar of his shirt; the crease of his trousers that was always flat out and k.o.'d at the knees; his very smile, which before did not stay on track and quickly wilted, bent, melted like an ice cube in the tropics; the tenuous side part of his hair; his slanted belt; the crooked stems of his glasses; even his gaze—all the sketchy, confused, unfinished, muddled segments of his body had been straightened, stiffened, and starched. The uncontrolled wires of his shapeless mustache had themselves been sheared into an impeccable realignment, a perfect, meticulously trimmed thread, as if traced Latin-style with a fine brush along his upper lip.

He and Ferrer considered each other a moment in silence. No doubt to give himself something to do, Delahaye began to twirl the glass in his hand gently on itself, then stilled his movement: the contents of the glass pursued their rotation alone before settling down in turn.

"Right," said Ferrer. "Why don't we go find a seat. It'll be easier to talk."

"Okay," sighed Delahaye.

They left the bar for the groups of deep armchairs, arrayed in threes and fours around covered pedestal tables. "Take your pick," said Ferrer. "I'm right behind you."

From there, as he followed, he observed the clothes worn by his former assistant: in this domain, too, Delahaye had changed. His anthracite-gray double-breasted flannel suit seemed to act as a back brace, so straight did the man now carry himself. As he turned to take a seat, Ferrer registered a midnight blue tie over a pearl-colored pinstripe shirt, oxfords the color of antique furniture on his feet, tie clip and cuff links emitting dull sparkles, muffled tones of muted opal and frosted gold—in short, he was dressed exactly as Ferrer had always wanted him to be at the gallery. The one flaw in the picture was when Delahaye dropped into a chair and the hems of his trousers lifted: the elastics of his socks seemed inordinately loose.

"You look really good like that," said Ferrer. "Where do you buy your clothes?"

"I didn't have anything left to wear," answered Delahaye. "I had to pick up a few things down here. You can find some great stuff in the center of town, you wouldn't believe how much cheaper it is than in France." Then he straightened in his chair, adjusted his tie, which had shifted slightly off-center—excess of emotion, no doubt—and pulled up the socks corkscrewed over his ankles.

"My wife gave me these socks," he added absently. "But they don't stay up, you see? They tend to fall down."

"Ah," Ferrer said, "that's pretty common. Socks people give you always fall down."

"That's true," Delahaye said with a tight smile. "That's an excellent observation. Can I buy you a drink?"

"With pleasure," said Ferrer. Delahaye signaled to a white jacket. They waited in silence for their order to arrive, then without smiling they raised their glasses and drank.

"Right," Delahaye then ventured. "What do we do now?"

"I'm not quite sure yet," said Ferrer. "That depends largely on you. Shall we go for a walk?"

They left the London & England Hotel and, instead of heading toward the ocean, which that evening seemed to be of violent disposition, took the opposite direction. The days began to shorten more and more frenetically; night thickened more and more quickly. They turned a corner onto Avenida de la Libertad, toward one of the bridges spanning the river.

Although this powerful waterway pours continuously into the Cantabrian sea, when the sea is too strong it flows back into the river, opposes and invades it; the fresh water chokes on so much bellicose salt. Then the countercurrents, after crashing against the piles of the Zurriola and Santa Catalina bridges, die down past the María Cristina bridge. Nonetheless they continue to shake the river, stirring it up below the surface, making the waters undulate as peristaltic movements do a stomach, as far as the Mundalz bridge and probably even farther. The two men stopped midway across the bridge. As they momentarily contemplated the war between insipid and salty being waged beneath them, and as Delahaye fleetingly recalled that he'd never learned how to swim, an idea crossed Ferrer's mind.

"I could get rid of you once and for all, when you get down to it," he said softly but without much conviction. "I could drown you, for example, it wouldn't be that hard. When you think about it, I probably *should*, for all the shit you've put me through."

As Delahaye hastily objected that such an action could only bring woe upon its perpetrator, Ferrer pointed out that since he had already disappeared officially, a second disappearance would surely pass unnoticed. "Everyone thinks you're dead," he reminded Delahaye. "You no longer have any legal existence. That's what you wanted, isn't it? So what risk would I be taking by eliminating you now? Killing a dead man isn't a crime," he supposed, not realizing he was reproducing the same logic that Delahaye had imposed on The Flounder.

"Come on, now," said Delahaye, "you're not going to do that."

"No," Ferrer allowed, "I don't believe so. Besides, I wouldn't know how to go about it. I'm not all that familiar with the techniques. Admit it, though, you fucked up."

"I admit it," said Delahaye. "Watch your language, but I admit that."

All this wasn't getting them very far, so for lack of arguments they fell silent for a minute or two. Ferrer wondered what had gotten into him to make him swear like that. Sometimes a stronger wave exploded noisily against a pile of the bridge, tossing fringes of foam as far as their shoes. The sugarloaf-shaped lamps of the María Cristina bridge projected an intimate glow. Upstream, they could see those of the Zurriola, shaped like ice-cream cones with three or four scoops, but which shed more light.

"So," Ferrer speculated calmly, "I could nail you for theft or larceny, fraud, what do I know. But theft is already illegal enough. I imagine passing yourself off for dead isn't terribly kosher either, do you think?"

"I wouldn't know," Delahaye responded. "I didn't really look into it."

"Besides, if you've already done that much," Ferrer said, "it probably didn't stop there. I suppose there's more I don't even know about." Remembering The Flounder's sad fate, Delahaye abstained from commenting on that supposition.

"All right," he said, "I blew it. All right, fine, I blew it. These things happen. But what am I going to do now, did you ever think of that? At the end of the day, you're the one who comes out of this smelling like roses," he added shamelessly. "You're still the one getting the better end of the deal."

With that, Ferrer shoved Delahaye against the guardrail, insulting him in a mutter, and began squeezing his throat without thinking. "You miserable little asshole," he then cried more distinctly. And losing all sense of restraint even after he'd scolded himself that same evening for using obscenities: "You sorry little fucked-up piece of shit"—while the other, head thrown back above the roiling waters, having tried to mouth a few obscenities himself, could now only gargle no, no, I'm begging you, no.

We have not taken the time, in the nearly one year that we've known him, to give a physical description of Ferrer. As this rather intense scene does not really lend itself to a long digression, we won't linger on it. Let's just say briefly that he's fairly tall, in his fifties, brown-haired with green eyes, or gray depending on the weather. Let's also say that he's not bad-looking, and let's specify that, despite his heart problems of all kinds and although he isn't particularly well-built, his strength can multiply when he gets worked up. That's what appears to be happening now.

"You pathetic shit-ass piece of garbage," he continued to shout, perilously compressing Delahaye's glottis, "fucking little shitty little two-bit swindler."

Cars passed over the bridge, a fishing boat glided underneath with lights off, four pedestrians ignoring their dispute fleetingly appeared on the opposite sidewalk, but no one stopped, despite the noise and the fact that it threatened to end badly. "No," Delahaye was now hiccuping, "please, no."

"Shut your face, asshole, just shut it," Ferrer spat

violently, "or you'll see how fast I can fucking shut it for you." And as the other started to go into convulsions, Ferrer felt his carotids beating frantically behind the angle of his jaw just as precisely as he'd seen his own arteries, several months earlier, during the electrocardiogram. "Jesus Christ!" he wondered all the while. "What's gotten into me tonight to swear like this?"

34

The days that followed ran their course in the usual order, having no alternative. First there was a whole day on the road, Ferrer having decided that he was in no hurry to return to Paris. Stopping for a leisurely lunch near Angoulême, allowing himself a detour of no particular scenic interest, just to give himself time to review and preview. In the car, which didn't have a signal scanner, he had to cruise the FM dial every sixty miles or so. It was, in any case, absently and at low volume that Ferrer listened to the radio, which served only as soundtrack to the film of the last twenty hours that he projected for himself in a continuous loop.

Things had gone almost too easily with Delahaye. After a moment of irritation, Ferrer had calmed down and they'd wound up negotiating. Delahaye, dazed and confused, found himself blocked at every turn. Nourishing great expectations for the clandestine sale of the antiques, anticipating enormous revenues, in the space of several months he had blown all his savings on luxury hotels and deluxe clothes: by now, he had almost nothing left. These expectations had been dashed by the arrival of Ferrer who, once he'd regained his senses, dragged him into a bar in the old town to propose a settlement. They had talked more calmly, looked to the future; Ferrer had gone back to addressing his old assistant in a more civil tongue.

For now, for lack of anything better, Delahaye decided to retain humbly and definitively the name Baumgartner, which he'd gone to great lengths to obtain: he would make of it what he could. He'd had to pay through the nose for it; false identity papers cost a bundle, and any backtracking was now impossible. He still tried to negotiate: for a compensatory sum, he would give up the address where the antiques were stored. Although Ferrer found his demands fairly benign, he took pleasure in talking him down, agreeing to pay him a little less than one-third the asking amount, which would be quite sufficient for Delahaye to manage awhile in the foreign country—with weak currency, if possible—of his choice. The other being in no position to bargain, they had settled matters there. They had finally parted company with no hard feelings, and Ferrer arrived back in Paris in the early evening.

The morning after his return, the first thing he did, on the strength of his former assistant's information, was go to Charenton to recover the objects; then he rented a large safe at the bank and wasted no time storing them, duly insured, inside it. That done, in the afternoon he went to Jean-Philippe Raymond's to pick up the final appraisal report; scarcely had he arrived at the reception than he ran into Sonia. Still the same with her Bensons and her Ericsson, which Ferrer could not help associating with the Babyphone. She made a show of looking him up and down with indifference, but, as he was following her in the hallway that led to Raymond's office, she suddenly spun around and bitterly reproached him for never having called. When Ferrer didn't answer, she began to insult him in a low voice, then, when he tried to create a diversion by ducking into the bathroom, she followed him in, threw herself into his arms, and ah, take me, she cried. He resisted, trying his best to impress upon her that it was neither the time nor the place, but she reacted violently and tried to scratch and bite him; then, abandoning all restraint, tried to unzip him on her knees intending to do goodness knows what, don't play innocent, you know perfectly well what. But, go figure, Ferrer fought her off. Restoring some measure of calm, he was able to escape these various assaults, not without mixed feelings. Luckily, a little later, back at the gallery, he noticed that in his absence things had evolved in a fairly positive direction. Business seemed to be picking up, but all afternoon Ferrer found it difficult to concentrate.

Sonia certainly wasn't the solution, but Ferrer, the man who has a hard time living without a woman, as we know, tried as of the next day but one to revive a few adventures. These were potential amours, flirtations put on the back burner or lures set in place long before, cases in progress, pending files offering greater or lesser degrees of interest. But none of his attempts panned out. The women who might have sparked his fancy turned out to be unreachable, now living elsewhere or otherwise engaged. Only the ones of minor interest appeared still viable, but then it was he who didn't give a damn.

Obviously there was still Hélène, although Ferrer hesitated to renew contact with her. He hadn't seen her since the day she'd worn makeup, having run off to Spain immediately afterward, and he still didn't have a very good idea of how to act around her or what to think. Too distant and too close, available and yet cold, opaque and smooth, she left few handholds for Ferrer to grab onto toward an unpredictable summit. He nonetheless resolved to call her, but even with Hélène he couldn't get a date for less than a week away. The week passed. After he had denied three times the temptation to cancel, everything happened according to the desperately common process, meaning that they had dinner then slept together; it wasn't a raging success but they did it. Then they did it again. It went a little better that time, so they tried it again and again until it became not bad at all, all the more so in that between those embraces they began to talk more spontaneously; it even happened that they laughed together. Things were moving forward. Perhaps they were moving forward.

Let's keep moving forward, too, and faster. In the weeks that follow, not only does Hélène come to spend more and more time on Rue d'Amsterdam, but she also frequents the gallery more and more often. Soon she has a spare key to the apartment. Soon Ferrer does not renew Elisabeth's contract and it is naturally Hélène who succeeds her, inheriting as well the keys to the gallery that Suzanne returned in front of the court-house.

Hélène learns the trade fairly quickly. She acquires so subtly the art of smoothing the edges that Ferrer entrusts her, part-time at first, with most of the deal-ings with his artists. Her tasks might include supervis-ing the evolution of Spontini's work, raising Gourdel's spirits, or moderating Martinov's pretensions. Her role is all the more necessary in that Ferrer is completely taken up by his recovered antiques.

Before long and naturally, without much having to be said about it, Hélène moves into Rue d'Amsterdam; then, with business going better and better, she is soon working full-time at the gallery. It seems the artists, Martinov in particular, would rather deal with her than Ferrer: she's calmer and more subtle than he, who every evening at Rue d'Amsterdam listens to her ac-count of the day. Although they have never really for-mulated any plans, it begins to look a lot like conjugal life. One can see them in the morning, she with her tea and he with his coffee, talking figures and publicity, manufacturing schedules, foreign exchanges, ending up definitively pulling the plug on the budget for the plastic artists.

Moreover, Ferrer is now thinking of moving. It's becoming entirely possible. The objects found in the *Nechilik* have yielded considerable profits, and besides, the market is on the rise these days. The telephone has begun ringing again, the collectors are opening a saurian eye, their checkbooks leap like roaches from their pockets. Eliminating the plastic artists has not lost them any revenue, while Martinov, for instance, is taking off toward the status of official painter: he's getting commissions for ministry foyers in London and factory entrances in Singapore, stage curtains and theater ceilings pretty much everywhere; his work is the subject of more and more retrospectives abroad, it's good, it's all good. Beucler and Spontini, the first to be surprised, also begin firmly consolidating their audiences, and even Gourdel, whom everyone had left for dead, has started selling again. Thanks to all this charming liquidity, Ferrer decides that they could, that they should, that they are going to change apartments. He is in a position to buy now: so they're going to find something bigger, something brand-new, a top floor in the middle of the sky that they've just finished building in the 8th arrondissement and that will be ready by mid-January.

While waiting for all the details of this residence to fall into place, they begin inviting people to Rue d'Amsterdam. They organize cocktail parties, dinner parties. They invite collectors like Réparaz, who comes without his wife, art critics and fellow gallery owners; one evening they even invite Supin, who shows up with his fiancée. In recognition of his help, Ferrer solemnly presents him with a small lithograph by Martinov that Hélène has managed to obtain below market value. Supin, very moved, at first declares that he can't accept, but he ends up leaving with his work of art wrapped up under one arm, his fiancé under the other. It is November, the air is dry and the sky blue; it's perfect. When they haven't invited anyone, sometimes they go out to eat, after which they have a drink at the Cyclone, the Central, the Sun, bars where they sometimes run into people from the same milieu, the same gallery owners or art critics they'd had over two nights before.

In the weeks that follow, up to the end of the month, it occasionally happens that Ferrer runs across—up close or, especially, at a distance—some of his old girlfriends. One day he spots Laurence waiting, like him, for the red light to turn green, at the other end of a zebra crossing near the Madeleine; but Ferrer, who recalls that their separation was not on the best of terms, prefers not to let her see him and sidles over to another stoplight to cross. Another time, on Place de l'Europe, he is suddenly engulfed in a wave of Extatics Elixir and sniffs it warily, but without managing to identify who is leaving it behind her. He's not certain it was Bérangère, for devotees of this perfume have, it seems, multiplied of late. He abstains from following this olfactory trail, which he never liked in any case, and avoids it altogether by slipping away in the opposite direction.

And one evening at the Central, where he has gone to have a drink with Hélène, Ferrer runs into Victoire, whom he hasn't seen since the beginning of the year. She looks basically the same, even though her hair is longer and her eyes more distant, as if their lenses had retracted to encompass a longer depth of field, a wider panorama. On top of which, she seems tired. They exchange a few meaningless words. Victoire seems distracted, but to the departing Hélène—"I'll leave you two for a moment," says Hélène, moving off—she gives the smile of a freed slave or vanquished conqueror. She doesn't seem to know about Delahaye's demise. Ferrer tells her the official version, with the appropriate sorrowful look, then buys her a glass of white wine and retreats after Hélène.

During that period, Ferrer prepares everything for his and Hélène's new apartment: their shared bedroom, as well as one for each of them when they'd rather sleep alone (best to plan for everything), the studies and guest bedrooms, kitchen and three bathrooms, terrace and hallways. Several times a week, he goes to visit the nearly completed construction site. He treads on raw concrete, breathing in the plaster dust that sticks to his palate as he envisions the trim and the paintings, the curtain colors and juxtapositions of furniture, without heeding the real estate agent who trips and stumbles among the girders while unfolding rough sketches. Hélène, meanwhile, prefers not to accompany Ferrer on his visits. Remaining at the gallery, she takes care of the artists, notably Martinov who has to be looked after closely, for success is such a fragile thing, it requires such constant attention, it's a never-ending job, while Ferrer, from the terrace of his future penthouse, watches the clouds gather.

Those clouds don't look so good, lined up and determined like a professional army. Moreover, the weather has turned suddenly, as if winter were losing patience, threatening to be in ill humor and shoving autumn aside with hostile gusts to take its place as soon as possible, choosing one hour of a late-November day to noisily despoil the branches of leaves that are shriveled to the state of mere memories. Climatically speaking, we have every reason to expect the worst.

35

So winter had arrived, and with it the end of the year, and with that its final eve, in view of which everyone had preventively made sure to invite each other back and forth. In the old days, the prospect of such evenings always made Ferrer a little nervous, but this time, not in the least. He had planned ahead, intending to take Hélène to Réparaz's where there was going to be a huge party: crowds of people, twelve bands and fourteen buffets, three hundred celebrities from every field, and two cabinet ministers for dessert. It promised to be a blast.

On the evening of the 31st, a little before the TV news, Ferrer was happily revealing this plan to Hélène when the doorbell rang. There stood the mailman, flanked by an assistant mailman, who had come for their year-end tip. They each carried a batch of complementary calendars with the obligatory pointing dogs, sleeping cats, birds on branches, seaside ports, and snowy peaks—an embarrassment of riches. "Of course," Ferrer said enthusiastically, "do come in."

Hélène seemed to agree with him as to the calendar selection. They opted for two recto-verso bouquets, one per half-year; in an excellent mood, Ferrer handed the mailmen three times their usual bonus. The enchanted postal workers wished the couple all possible happiness; Ferrer heard them commenting on the event in the stairway as he shut the door behind them, but, that done, Hélène announced that she had something to say. "Of course," said Ferrer. "What is it?" Well, she said, about that party at Réparaz's—actually, she'd rather not go. Martinov was also having a little get-together with a few friends in his new studio, the fruit of all his recent sales and of a size better suited to his current standing, and there you had it, that was where she wanted to spend her evening. If you don't mind.

"Not at all," said Ferrer, "whatever you like." Of course it would be a bit delicate given his relations with Réparaz, but he'd think of something, it shouldn't be that hard to cancel.

"The thing is, no," said Hélène, turning away, "that's not what I meant." All things considered, it was better if she went alone. And as Ferrer pursed his lips and knitted his brow: "Listen," Hélène said, turning back to him, "listen." She explained gently that she had thought about it. This new apartment. All that furniture. The thought of living together with all that sky above them. She wasn't really sure. She wasn't sure she was ready, she needed to think about it, they should talk about it some more. "I'm not saying we should let it drop, you know? I'm just saying I need to think about it some more. Let's take a few days and talk it over then."

"Fine," said Ferrer, examining the toes of his new shoes—new, as of several weeks ago, as all his shoes were—"fine, all right."

"You're sweet," said Hélène. "I'm going to go change now. You can tell me all about Réparaz's."

"Yeah," said Ferrer, "I don't know."

She left Rue d'Amsterdam—a little early, he judged, for that kind of evening. Left alone and pacing a moment around the living room, turning on the television only to turn it off immediately afterward, Ferrer spontaneously cursed Feldman for having forbidden him to smoke. Then he made two or three halfhearted phone calls, reached as many answering machines. No longer really felt like going to Réparaz's, who, having gotten to like Hélène since she started working at the gallery, would surely wonder about her absence. Having obviously made no other plans for the evening, he was now at a loss to improvise an emergency backup. All the more so in that, having declined other invitations, phoning casually to latch on at the last minute would be delicate: there, too, people would wonder, ask questions that he did not have the slightest wish to answer.

He made several more calls, in greater number but crowned with the same results. He slipped a disc into the CD player, immediately lowered the volume, tried another disc, muted the sound on the television the second he turned it on, then stood in front of it for a long while without changing channels or understanding what he was seeing. He also remained standing for several minutes in front of the open refrigerator, in the same cataleptic state and without removing a single item. And now two hours later, here he is walking down Rue de Rome toward the Saint-Lazare metro stop, from where it's a direct line to Corentin-Celton.

On December 31st at 11 P.M., the subway cars are generally not overcrowded. It's not unusual to find entire benches empty the way Ferrer likes them, he who is well aware of choosing at this moment quite possibly the worst of all solutions.

Ferrer knows that Suzanne, left exactly one year minus two days ago, is a past master at New Year's Eve festivities. He also knows that he's exposing himself to the worst and that this worst would be justified. He knows even more that Suzanne might react violently to the sight of him, that the whole thing is extremely risky. It might even qualify as a suicide operation, but it seems he doesn't care, as if there were nothing else to be done, I know it's crazy but I'm doing it anyway. And besides, you never know, maybe Suzanne has changed; maybe she's become civilized since their first meeting. It's just that she has always been a neolithically violent person, and Ferrer sometimes wonders if he didn't meet her at the mouth of a cave: Suzanne holding a club in one hand, a flint hatchet stuck in her belt. That day she was wearing a pterodactyl-wing suit under a trench coat cut from an ichthyosaur's eyelid, and sporting an iguanodon's nail fitted to the shape of her head. It hadn't been easy over the following five years, they'd waged quite a few battles, but perhaps things have evolved; we'll see.

The house has changed, in any case. Like the latch on the gate, the mailbox is repainted red; its label no longer bears Ferrer's name, nor Suzanne's maiden name. Since every window is lit, it seems the house is now occupied by new tenants celebrating the end of the year. Disconcerted, Ferrer remains near the gate for a few moments, without the slightest idea of what he is going to do nor wants to do, until the front door opens and out comes a burst of loud music and a girl who stands in the doorway, not seeming to want to leave, by all appearances only out for a breath of air.

She seems nice enough; catching sight of him, she gives him a little wave and a smile. She has a glass in her hand and is about twenty-five or thirty, not too bad-looking, sort of a lesser Bérangère. It isn't too unlikely that she's also slightly drunk, but only slightly, which is hardly a crime at this sort of gathering. As Ferrer continues to lurk near the gate, she calls out to him, "Are you a friend of George's?"

Ferrer, highly embarrassed, does not answer immediately. "Suzanne isn't there, by chance, is she?" he finally asks.

"I don't know," says the girl. "I haven't seen any Suzannes, but maybe she's here. There are a lot of people inside. I don't know them all. I'm the sister of one of George's business partners—he just moved in. The house is pretty nice, but it's so hot in there."

"Yes," says Ferrer, "it seems nice."

"Would you like to come in for a drink?" the girl offers kindly.

Behind her, through the open door, Ferrer can see the repainted entrance, different furniture, an unfamiliar lamp, images hanging or pinned to the wall that neither he nor Suzanne would have owned. "Okay, sure," he says. "But I don't want to be any trouble."

"Not at all," the girl says, smiling. "Come in."

"I'm really sorry," says Ferrer, approaching cautiously. "This isn't what I expected. It's a bit difficult to explain."

"No problem," says the girl. "I didn't plan to be here either. There are some really nice people inside, you'll see. Come on, come on in."

"All right," says Ferrer, "but I'm only staying a moment. Just one drink and then I'm going."